THE Broken MIRACLE

— PART ONE —

J.D. NETTO

THE

Broken

MIRACLE

—— PART ONE ——

Cover design © 2021 by J.D. Netto Designs
Book design and production by J.D. Netto Designs
Edited by HubEdits
Piano and mountain photo: Shutterstock

To my mother, who taught me to believe in the impossible.

from

Paul Cardall

It's a bit surreal to hold a novel inspired by my own life. I know my journey hasn't been the easiest or what people consider "normal," but seeing some of the most challenging moments I lived translated into words on a page brought clarity to many questions I had.

The experience of having an author put together a puzzle that was often just a pile in my head brought light to my own shadows. The book puts into words many things I tried to voice throughout my life. It portrays the emotions and downfalls I experienced while many around me seemed healthy and strong.

My personal contribution is burrowed in each chapter. I got to edit each scene with notes from my personal experiences. Seeing them expand into powerful moments in the story was a breath of fresh air—even for me. It brought me perspective, healing, and even more courage to keep on living.

My hope is that this novel instills in you the desire to live. I've been on the brink of death countless times, thought about giving up in a few of them, but in the end, love prevailed. I'm alive. My heart is beating. Life is worth living.

 www.facebook.com/PaulCardallMusic

 www.instagram.com/PaulCardall

 www.PaulCardall.com

from

J.D. Netto

I was in my hotel room in Seattle in 2010 when the song "Redeemer" came on. I was engrossed in its melody as soon as the string arrangements began. There was something about the song that made me quickly search the internet for the genius behind it. I stumbled upon the name "Paul Cardall" and his remarkable story of living with half a heart.

He became a constant presence in my playlists, his songs the soundtrack of some of my most personal moments. I downloaded every album and religiously visited iTunes hoping for new content. To my surprise (I still pinch myself to this very day), on February 2019, I was presented with the chance of writing the novel you now hold in your hand.

These books changed my life. Not only because I got to work with one of my inspirations, but because the journey is one that dares you to believe against all odds. It's a roller coaster where those riding can't see the tracks. They're only sure of the drop, but confused as to where it'll lead.

 www.facebook.com/JDNettoOfficial

 www.instagram.com/JDNetto

 www.JDNetto.com

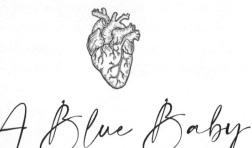

A Blue Baby

JULY 2005

I belonged to an exclusive club with only one membership requirement—be born with half a functioning heart. I felt like a lucky dog every time I removed the leash that was my oxygen tubes in the morning. Normal for me was waking up with two thick lines carved on my cheeks that sometimes remained visible throughout the day. I chose to see them as my reward for a good night's sleep. Or for just being alive.

My wife, Olivia, was in our bed beside me, eyes closed, her brown tresses strewn on the pillow. She had a beauty mark on her right cheek, right above her lips. Twelve-hour night shifts at the hospital usually kept her asleep until early afternoon.

I sat up on the edge of the bed, hand on my chest. "Well, you're still working." Tom Sawyer beat against my hand. Yes, I named my heart Tom Sawyer—Sawyer for short. Mark Twain would approve, Huck Finn would be jealous, and my favorite rock band, Rush, would be proud since, in my opinion, "Tom Sawyer" was their best song. Every time I listened to their drummer's patterns, I thought of Sawyer and how, against all odds, he kept on beating. After countless doctor appointments, procedures, and surgeries, I decided to give it a name so I could see it as a friend—a very broken friend.

Olivia turned over in her sleep, pregnant belly pointing toward me. The sight earned a wide smile from me.

Whenever I looked at her baby bump, I often imagined the despair my parents felt when they were told about my condition. It can't be easy knowing your newborn will need heart surgery a few hours after being held for the first time. Most people will never experience that as parents; I prayed to be one of those people.

For obvious reasons, I don't remember anything that happened at the hospital on April 24, 1973. From what I was told, my mom's labor and my arrival were pretty routine stuff until they saw me. I was a "blue baby," a nickname given to children born with a lack of oxygen in their blood. I'd like to think my lips were so blue that medical personnel thought I inherently belonged to some metal band, but considering the dire situation that day, I don't think they had much time for sarcasm.

Cardiologists at Salt Lake County Hospital transported me to the Primary Children's Medical Center, where I had my first heart catheterization.

Sawyer was diagnosed with double inlet left ventricle. A normal heart has two ventricles and two atriums designed to receive blood. Oxygen-poor blood flows into the right atrium and ventricle before being sent to the pulmonary artery, where vessels carrying the blood to the lungs pick up oxygen. The oxygenated blood returns through the left atrium and ventricle and is distributed to the rest of the body. The only functioning ventricle Sawyer had was the left one, forcing my two atriums to spew blood together like two chemicals never meant to be mixed.

The story goes that my dad and grandfather got permission to take me into a custodian's closet on the way to surgery, where they prayed for divine intervention. We want God to just wave His hand and work a miracle, but often times the miracle is God laying the puzzle pieces down and watching us figure out how to put them together. He's no wizard waving about a wand but, rather, an architect slowly revealing a blueprint.

I underwent my first major heart surgery twenty-two hours after I was born. A gifted surgeon created a connection between my left ventricle and aorta, the large artery that supplies blood to the lower part of the body. This helped increase the oxygen in my blood as it flowed from my lungs.

Though the open-heart surgery was successful, my parents were told if I lived out my first year, I'd need several more surgeries at some point in the future. Luckily, after thirty-two years, Sawyer was still around, beating my life away. But the deepening dark circles around my eyes and waning weight were constant reminders of how sick he was.

After brushing my teeth, I walked out of our bedroom and was immediately greeted by the unpainted walls in the room across the hall. It was to be our baby boy's bedroom. Olivia had already picked the color for the walls, but I kept postponing painting them. I wanted to hold on to every moment of this pregnancy—especially after all our miscarriages.

Normally, I'd press play on my iPod and wait to see what song came out of the stereo speakers in the kitchen. But this morning, I was in the mood for Rush. I listened to "The Spirit of Radio" while eating my bowl of Cocoa Puffs and a slice of banana bread. The music brought me back to my teenage days, and even though much of it consisted of surgeons, nurses, and needles, there were still plenty of good memories mixed in.

My younger brother and I would listen to the trio all the time. Jonahs was the only other songwriter in the family aside from me. The difference was that to Jonahs, music was a hobby, but to me it was my whole life—my love and livelihood.

I went to the living room after breakfast and sat at the piano. It faced the window for a better view of Salt Lake City's most recognizable sight. The city had been built in a valley, separated by the Wasatch Mountains to the east and the Oquirrh Mountains to the west. Amidst the encircling mountain ranges, one could be seen throughout the entire city. For me, the landscape of Mount Olympus, set apart from other formations by its twin peaks and outcroppings, always inspired new music. A songwriter couldn't ask for a better muse.

When I started performing, the mall was my usual venue. I'd play for hours and was lucky enough to sell most of my CDs. Those were the days when I began to realize my music could actually take me somewhere. And that night, I was performing at Assembly Hall on Temple Square, the most popular tourist attraction in Salt Lake City. For better or worse, I was about to experience one of the most monumental moments of my career. Whether it was a packed house full of fans or a handful of neighbors and my parents, it would be unforgettable.

I looked out at Mount Olympus for a few more seconds and got on with practice. My right hand lifted from my lap, fingers striking the keys. A melody echoed. My left hand joined in and the music rescued me. A close friend died when I was a teenager. It was his friendship that sparked the desire in me to play, but it was his death that actually got me to begin. The better I got, the more I realized music helped me cope with things like death. Like Sawyer.

Here I was doing it again. Me, the mountains, and my music. The music let me forget I was down to 150 pounds. It let me forget most of that weight was me retaining fluid. It let me forget I was losing oxygen in my blood. It was always this void—this lack—that I filled with each note.

I spotted Olivia standing in her light blue nightdress. Her shoulder rested on the doorway, pregnant belly in sight.

"Oh, sorry." My hands retreated to my lap, the last note, a C in the lower register, echoing around the room. "I didn't mean to wake you. Was I being too loud?"

She smiled. "Don't worry, I don't think I'll be able to get any sleep this morning anyway." She sat beside me, giving me a peck on the cheek.

"Sorry, sweetheart." I kissed her beauty mark, my attention shifting to her belly. "Good morning, you!" I caressed the baby bump with an unstoppable smile.

"Well, at least *he* gets to sleep," she said, making us both laugh.

"How was the hospital?" I asked.

"Just another day. I don't think I'll ever get used to seeing mothers say goodbye to their newborns." She shook her head in dismissal. "But I don't want to talk about that stuff." She took in a quick breath. "Nervous about tonight?"

"More like worried." I chuckled. "What if people don't show? Imagine how monumental it would be"—I held up my hands, forming the shape of a rectangle in the air—"*Paul Cardall plays to an empty Assembly Hall.*"

"Knowing you, you'd still play your songs to an empty room."

"Like I was doing before you walked in?" I smirked.

She laid a hand on my shoulder. "Everything will be fine."

"Yeah, yeah," I said. "Of course it will."

"And listen, if you think the audience is getting bored, just play an Elvis cover on the piano and you'll be golden."

"Let me guess the song suggestion," I said behind a laugh. "'Can't Help Falling in Love?'"

She gave me a peck on the lips. "You are correct."

"I'll add your favorite song to the list in case of a concert emergency."

"Have you heard from Jonahs?" she asked.

"I did. He seemed better last week. But I suppose he's still getting back to normal. Hard to say."

"Is he coming tonight?"

"No." I cleared my throat. "It's too soon for anything like that."

She squeezed my hand. "Tell you what, you keep on playing, I'm going to shower and then run out."

"Want me to come and inspect your work?" I asked, hoping to get my mind off the concert with a little romance.

"Ha-ha very funny." She raised my chin with a finger. "You'll be great tonight."

"Yeah," I mumbled. "Not even a two-minute make out session?" My brows arched up.

"Let's focus." She pecked me on the forehead and, defeated, I watched her retreat upstairs.

I returned to the piano. Seeing Olivia pregnant had inspired some of my best melodies. I imagined what my days would be like with a little boy around. I had never heard his voice, but lately I was combining notes I imagined would sound like his laugh. I pictured tiny soul-piercing eyes and how much of an honor being a dad would be.

But we'd already had two miscarriages. There was no way to look forward without remembering where we'd been.

Olivia was five months along. I knew the risk she took when she decided to build a family with me. Her father advised her not to. He said he didn't want her life turning out like his. He'd cared for her mother when she fell ill with cancer. I once overheard him say that no matter how much she loved me, choosing me would leave her walking toward the same cliff he had.

Her mother's cancer was the downfall of her siblings. Many resorted to drugs and alcohol for comfort, leading to years of suffering and misery. I'm sure she feared the same fate awaited our family if I didn't make it—a life full of cracks and holes and questions.

A dark progression of notes turned the light song I played into a somber hymn. For a moment, the music showed me my son mourning his father's early death. Olivia beside him over my graveside, regretting the decision to have ever loved me, wishing her heart could've loved someone else.

I didn't fear death. I only worried about its aftermath for my family.

I've learned how limited our time on Earth is over and over since childhood. When I was nine, a kid in town named Spencer died of cancer. Before he passed, we prayed, raised money, fasted, and did all the godly things we were supposed to do. He still died.

It was funny how this "curse" of mine had the power to inspire me. Sawyer was broken. Badly. My clock ticked a little differently. And it was the constant reminder of the shortness of my life that motivated me to defy the odds.

Even if death whispered in my ear every once in a while, I refused to be remembered as the one who was defeated by Sawyer. I wanted to be remembered as the one who fought the good battle. That was the hopeful spirit I was going to play with at my concert. That was the life I needed to live.

Deep Waters

JULY 1986

"Ready for the big day?" Mom asked, hands on the steering wheel, the top of her freshly permed hair in view from the backseat. "Fly by Night" by Rush played on the stereo now that she had finally allowed me to choose the music.

"I mean, I'm ready to surprise any stranger who asks why I have a scar under my right armpit," I replied with a grin.

I thought Dad had believed in me a bit too much when he signed me up for the National Scout Jamboree and got me started with this whole Eagle Scout business. Dad claimed he had such a great time when he did it that I should also get to experience it. Of course, I said yes to the whole thing. A part of me was afraid of what I had gotten myself into. If it was already hard for the other guys, imagine how it would be for me.

"I'm serious," Mom said, rolling her eyes. "You've trained so hard."

"Not just trained." I counted off with my fingers. "Trained, suffered, and almost drowned."

"Oh, please." She smiled. "You loved every minute of it. But if you don't survive, we'll just give all the records and cassettes you bought with your paper route money to your siblings."

"No, no. If I don't make it, you'll give them all to Jonahs. And that's my final wish," I said. "I'm sure he'll appreciate my collection more than the rest of them."

She laughed. "Done."

"But seriously, they had me jumping in the deep end and then they told me to make a flotation device out of my clothes," I said, scratching the back of my neck. I loved my Goonies t-shirt, but the tag always felt like sand rubbing on my skin.

"But you made it through, didn't you?" Her diamond eyes glanced at me through the mirror.

"I knew I would And honestly, I think Coach Dave enjoys watching us struggle in the water."

"Why do you say that?" She lowered the volume of the music as a frown appeared on her face.

"Because a whole bunch of boys making flotation devices out of their clothes in the deep end of a cold swimming pool is a classic example of a corny summer camp movie." I shrugged. "He gets to watch us suffer while getting paid for it."

"You *do* remember he's a friend of ours, right?"

"Then that makes him our lazy friend," I said snidely.

"I'll be sure to tell him that." A laugh followed. "Your dad is very proud of you. You're setting such an example to your siblings and cousins. They see what you do and want to do the same."

"Gee, thanks, Mom. Just remind them I still have to survive today. And even if I do, I won't even be an Eagle Scout yet. There's still a long journey ahead."

"You'll be fine," she said with a wave of dismissal, turning the radio back up.

Mom was the honorary driver and disc jockey to all my destinations. She made the rides more fun by taking the hills a little faster, so when we went over the bumps, I got butterflies in my stomach like on a roller coaster. I honestly loved my parents—I knew it was a rare thing for a thirteen-year-old to say, but it was the truth. They never treated me differently because of my heart. They just boasted that I was a living miracle. I felt bad for my seven siblings whenever they were reminded that anything was possible if Paul's heart was still beating.

"Let's do this!" Mom said excitedly as she parked in front of my future high school, Mount Olympus High. Her brown dress stamped with yellow flower patterns flowed in the breeze when she got out of the car.

"Did you bring your pompoms, too?" I asked.

"No, just a shirt with your face on it," she replied, locking the doors.

We entered the school, Mom's hair bouncing with her every step as she commented on all the posters and class projects hung on the walls.

I was greeted by the other boys when we entered the indoor pool area, where we were told our mission for the day was to swim a mile without stopping. Well, except for me. I was allowed to hold on to the edge of the pool when needed.

Mom and I parted ways. I headed to the locker room to change, and she made her way to the bleachers.

Coach Dave stopped me before I could reach my destination. "How are we feeling, Paul?" He wore a cardigan sweater despite the 80-degree weather, bald head reflecting the light from the tall glass windows.

"As ready as I'll ever be." I frowned at his thick, foggy glasses.

"Good." He took the glasses off and wiped the lenses on his sweatshirt. "Very proud of you, kid. And remember, if you're feeling tired—"

"Don't worry. I won't drop dead in the middle of the pool," I said as he put his glasses back on, fixing them on top of his nose. "And if I spot the Loch Ness Monster, I can always use that curly mustache of yours to help me float."

"Very funny." He nodded. "Go get ready."

I entered the locker room and quickly put on my swim shorts, but the reflection of my massive scar pulled me to a stop on my way out. It was long, streaking from my left armpit all the way to my back, underneath my shoulder blade.

I placed a hand over my chest. "Don't fail me today... please, please, please, please."

I walked out to meet the others and approached the edge of the Olympic-sized pool. Mom waved proudly once she spotted me. I returned the gesture with a thin smile. For a second, I wondered if I made a mistake in thinking I could do this. I looked at the other boy scouts, knowing they were going to finish their laps way before me, and then glanced at the spectators on the bleachers. Many probably didn't know who I was. What would they think of the boy coming last? I knew, at the very least, my scar would inspire some pity in them. And I hated that.

"Alright, everyone jump in!" A blaring whistle followed Coach Dave's loud voice.

We dove in, the water too freaking cold for an indoor pool. With every kick of my feet and move of my arms, I was reminded of how unqualified I was.

I kept pace with the others for a lap and a half, Sawyer fluttering wildly, before my lungs suddenly craved air, and my muscles decided to go on vacation. Heavy breaths replaced my optimism. I held on to the edge of the pool, watching the other boys continue. After resting for a few seconds, I carried on swimming only to have my body start shutting down again.

I kept repeating the cycle. Hold the edge. Swim a little. Hold the edge. Swim a little. People would be surprised at how much of a workout that was. Though a part of me worried what the others thought, I was determined to finish regardless of the cost.

The other scouts were already wrapped in towels, standing by the edge of the pool laughing and goofing around. They were done. I was still dragging and swimming, wondering if I was going to finish. But every lap was already a victory. Everyone else could wait a little longer.

Suddenly, every single one of Sawyer's frantic beats turned into victory horns. I laughed the moment I finished my last lap. I climbed out, my body shaking, my fingers wrinkled like shriveled prunes.

Dave approached me, a high five at the ready. "You did it, kid."

I slapped his palm with my own. "Yeah," I said behind heavy breaths, lowering my hand to my thumping chest.

I looked over my shoulder, surveying the empty pool and the crowd on the bleachers.

I did it. I finished.

Coming Full Circle

JULY 2005

Olivia and I arrived at the Assembly Hall early. After being greeted at the back door, we were led to the green room. She had my suit jacket in hand, holding the hanger by the hook.

"Pretty surreal that we're here." Olivia said with wide eyes, closing the door behind us. "We're actually backstage. Can you believe it?"

I laughed and told her to pinch me. My reflection appeared in the wide mirror on the wall to my right, gelled hair reflecting the scattered light. "I heard we have a full house. Who would've thought?"

"I don't think you'll need that emergency Elvis song tonight," she said, handing me my navy-blue suit jacket with a thin smile. My eyes scanned her body's figure as I put it on, admiring the way her dress accentuated her curves.

"Still can't believe we're here."

"I'm so proud." Her hazel eyes looked down as she caressed her belly. "Are you proud of your dad, too?"

"Fingers crossed he is," I said, gaze fixed on her face.

In front of the mirror was a long wooden table crowded with trays of fruit and cheese. Beside them were red plastic cups and soda bottles.

After pulling out a chair for Olivia, she sat down and reached for the bottle of Diet Coke. "I'm not even going to ask which one you want," she said, twisting the cap.

"It's a shame they only have one bottle." I sat beside her, observing our reflection.

Maybe it was the lighting in the room, but my dark circles looked like charcoal smudges, adding a touch of gray to my blue eyes. My cheeks were puffed, my skin flushed. But Sawyer was still pounding.

"Being here is full circle for me." She slid a red cup of Diet Coke over and then poured herself one. A long sigh followed. "I never told you, but Mom played piano here before she died."

"Really?" I said, body suddenly numb.

"Sorry if this is a bit out of nowhere. It's just that being here is sparking all sorts of emotions." She took a sip from her cup. "It's a sad thing to say, but when I think of her, I only remember sickness and pain." She fixed her brown locks behind her ears, pursing her lips. "I'd watch my siblings help her to the bathroom so she could vomit after her treatments. I was three. It was horrible."

She had shared a few things about her mom's disease in the past. But Olivia's days with her dying mother were somewhat of a mystery. She often chose not to talk about them. Her dad had been my main source of information for that time.

Her eyes met mine in the mirror. "In the few good memories I have of her, I hear her voice whispering, 'Seeing the cup half full paves the way for many blessings.' I'd look at her every time she repeated it, wondering how someone in her condition could keep saying that."

"How come you never told me?" I asked as she rose to her feet.

"Some things are just for me. That was one of them," she replied as a frown formed on her face. "Funny how life works, right?" The corners of her lips trembled. "You always want to avoid painful situations, and plenty of times that's exactly how you get placed right in the middle of them. You choose to believe in some sort of miracle only to be disappointed in the end."

"What do you mean?" Sawyer rushed his pace.

"I used to believe Mom would get better. But then she played here and died." Her eyes grew vacant. "Now you're playing here and—"

A knock.

"Hello!" Dad appeared from behind the door.

"Hey, you!" Mom emerged beside him, both of them wearing their Sunday best.

"Hey." I got up and gave them a hug, Olivia's words playing out in my head. "You guys are early."

"You know how much your dad dislikes looking for parking," Mom said.

We all shared a laugh. "I see you're stocked up on food." Dad circled the table, carefully inspecting the choices on display.

"Help yourself to anything you want," Olivia said, struggling to keep her emotions from showing on her face.

"How's the baby?" Dad asked, a few grapes in hand.

"Very good," Olivia replied. "Growing."

Dad nodded before turning to me. "And how are you?"

"I'm good. I keep thinking about this hall." I put my hands in my pockets. "I mean, there's a Steinway Model D on stage. That alone would have made me happy even if no one showed up."

"The finest piano for the finest son," he said in a serious voice. "Congratulations."

"Thanks. I wish Jonahs was here to see this. I'd find a way to sneak in a few bars of Rush for him."

"There'll be other opportunities," Dad said.

"He called, by the way." Mom reached for a slice of

cheddar. "Wished you good luck."

"Thank you," I said. "I'll give him a ring tomorrow."

"Alright, Maggie, we should head inside." Dad grabbed an apple.

"Be honest; you only came early for the free food." I chuckled.

"How did you guess?" Mom smiled after taking a cracker.

"Good luck, Son," Dad said.

"Bye, you two." Mom waved. "It'll be great."

I returned to my chair after they left, lacing my fingers over the table. Olivia kept pacing around the room.

"You can sit back down."

"I'm alright." She nibbled on the corner of her thumb.

"I want you to know I'll make it through this ordeal," I declared.

She halted and looked at me, confused. "I'm sure you'll be amazing tonight."

"No, I mean I'm going to beat the odds of this jacked up heart."

A few members of the backstage crew entered the room, interrupting us, and Olivia left soon after.

The moment I walked onstage, the crowd stood and applauded. They weren't there to see some random artist or because they felt sorry for the man with half a heart. They knew me. They knew my music. They knew my journey. The crowd reminded me of the pool and how hard I'd worked to finish my laps. How, even if I had to cling to the edge, I could accomplish my goals.

Peace came to me as I played. I looked around the room and could somehow feel a divine power wrapping a blanket around those present. But even in the middle of such a glorious moment, in the back of my mind, Olivia's words echoed like haunting lyrics to my melodies.

"She played here and died. Now you're playing here."

Brothers (part one)

JULY 2005

Jonahs called the day after the concert, apologizing for not making it. I told him not to worry, but he insisted on me coming up to the family cabin on Saturday so we could go fishing. I quickly agreed, thinking he probably needed to talk after what happened to him. He had yet to broach the subject since being sent home from the hospital.

After a week of working on my new album, *Primary Worship*, and shopping for baby stuff, I was on my way to Pines Ranch in full fly fishing armor: a vest packed with supplies, beige waders, and pull-on wading boots with new felt on the base so I wouldn't slip on the rocks. The thirty-minute drive inspired me to be bold and roll down my windows in the Utah summer. My courage lasted for as long as it took me to start sweating. I rolled the windows back up, and blasted the A/C, along with a Rush song from the CD I had burned especially for the weekend.

Pine trees stretched far beyond my line of sight, and snow

covered the mountain peaks on the horizon. I drove slowly. Distractedly; the memory of Olivia's rigid face and those haunting words sparking all my doubts. My attention switched between the road and a photo stuck to the car's dashboard of Olivia and me. In the picture, we smiled at each other. If a stranger were to glance at it, unaware of my story, they'd think we were just an ordinary couple.

Sawyer pounded faster against my ribcage as the conversation replayed in my head like a piano scale—up and down, up and down, back and forth. Maybe, deep down, she wished she'd listened to her dad and not chosen me.

I feared being right and shoved those thoughts away.

After turning off the highway, I drove another half a mile until coming to a dirt road. I lowered the music at the sight of the cabin gates, the words *Pines Ranch* suspended in an arch.

The dense pine forest had been replaced by a vast field of grass crowded with grazing horses and skipping foals. Driving down the dirt road brought me back to my childhood. This place was stuck in time, never changing—a reminder of simpler days.

The cabin, built by my father and uncles, was in full view as I pulled around the final curve. Mountains peaked behind it, their summits disappearing into clouds. Jonahs emerged from the door before I even parked. I rolled down the window as he rushed my way.

"I thought you were never going to make it," he said, a red

plaid shirt, blue jeans, and boots his outfit of choice. Jonahs insisted on keeping a short buzz cut and a stub of a beard.

"What are you talking about?" My hands abandoned the steering wheel, falling to my lap.

"You drive like an old lady, Paul." He shrugged. "It's either that, or you took the long route."

His voice faded as I turned up the music, banging my head to Rush's "YYZ."

Jonahs shook his head, clearly disapproving of my brief rebellion. I shut off the car and opened the door. His arms wrapped around me before my feet could even hit the ground.

"Good to see you too," I said.

"Same." He looked me up and down. "You look good," he said, tilting his head to the side, a common gesture after people complimented me. I wondered if they knew their faces didn't match their words. But then, I knew my appearance shocked them.

"Thanks." I tapped my stomach. "Keeping the weight off, you know."

"Very funny." More disapproval followed. "And hey, sorry I couldn't make it to the concert. Really wanted to."

"No worries." My arm hooked around his shoulders. "I'm just happy you're alright."

"So, you drove here dressed in full gear." He snickered. "Tell me, is my famous musician brother so short on cash he can't afford luggage and has to wear all his gear?"

"I've barely arrived, and you're already testing my patience," I said. "I'll be honest, I think the only reason you keep shaving your head is because you know you're going to be bald in five years."

My words earned a smile. "Come on," he said. "Hannah cooked lunch. It's probably already cold since it took you forever to get here."

"What can I say?" I smirked. "I followed the speed limit."

"The words of a person lacking an adventurer's spirit." He leapt up the steps to the porch, standing with hands on his waist and legs spread out like a superhero.

The inviting smell of a home-cooked meal filled my nose as I neared the door. Hannah appeared in the doorway, her blonde hair tied back and an old white apron around her waist. "What's up, Pollyanna?" she said with a smile. "I hope you're hungry. We've been waiting an eternity for you, but glad to see you finally made it."

"I'm flattered you'd wait an eternity for me." I chuckled as Jonahs closed the door behind me. "And yes, I'm starving. It smells amazing."

"Now you're just being too nice, Paulie," she said. "Give me some time to set the table. You want something to drink?"

"You guys have any diet soda?" I sat on the couch.

"We knew you were coming," Hannah said. "There's plenty of Diet Coke for you."

"Water for me, honey." Jonahs sat next to me. "Unlike some people, I don't enjoy drinking poison."

There were family photos scattered everywhere, surrounded by oil paintings of mountains and landscapes. On the mantel of the fireplace was a framed photo Jonahs took of the cabin. He edited it to look like a photograph taken last century, adding texture and removing some of the colors. On the coffee table beside me was an old portrait of Jonahs and me as kids, riding horses with our siblings, Dan, Janet, and Greg.

"This is new." I grabbed the frame. "Wasn't this the week we forgot you when we went to church?"

"I think so." He laughed. "That was an interesting day."

Hannah brought the drinks and quickly returned to the dining room. Still holding the picture frame, I chanced a question I had never asked before.

"What went through your head?" I put the frame back and took a big gulp from the cold can. "When you realized we were all gone?"

"It's human to forget."

"I don't think it's very human to forget someone," I retorted.

"I wasn't *forgotten* by you guys," he said. "I was simply left behind. If I had really been forgotten, Mom wouldn't have come back to pick me up."

I kept my eyes on the frame. "You never really spoke about it. You also ended up missing church."

"Lunch is on the table." Hannah's voice startled me.

"Enough of this." Jonahs finished his water and darted to his feet. "Time to eat some grub," he said, walking to the kitchen.

I glanced at the portrait beside me one more time, the picture a reminder of simpler days, when our parents would tell us what to do, and we obeyed. Well, some of us. Even then, Jonahs tended to look at the world with curious eyes. Sure, curiosity was a gift, but being too curious could be dangerous.

I talked about the concert, Olivia, and our baby boy during lunch. They insisted I tell them the name, but I refused, promising the suspense would be worth it. Jonahs talked about college and the excitement of finally moving to Arizona with Hannah and starting his PhD. No one mentioned what happened to Jonahs a few weeks ago—the three of us clearly wanting to forget. But you could sense the subject lingering around us and all through the cabin, waiting to find its way into the conversation. Maybe what happened to him was a result of bottling up too much and speaking too little.

After we were done eating, Hannah brought out home-made ice cream and some bottles of root beer.

"No lunch is complete without dessert." She set it on the table.

"Oh, man." I placed a hand over my chest. "I hope he won't

punish me for indulging a little bit."

"You'll be fine," Jonahs said. "And you can't use the excuse that you're too bloated so you can ditch me and go home early."

"Don't you see my outfit? You think I go around wearing this every day? Did you think this was a fashion statement?" My hand landed on his shoulder. "You may be a genius, and I may love you and all, but it was the fish that made me come here."

We all shared a laugh and reveled in our ice cream and root beer like children.

"Come to the shed." Jonahs pushed his chair away from the table and jumped to his feet as soon as he finished the last bit of his float. "Come on!"

"Can I finish mine first?" My right eyebrow turned into an arch.

"Sure." He stared like a kid looking at candy.

"Fine, fine!" I finished mine up with a single slurp. "Happy?" I asked, ice cream dripping from the corners of my lips.

"Very. Now, come on!" He banged a hand on the table.

I rolled my eyes, grabbing a napkin to wipe my lips, before turning to Hannah. "You need help washing up?"

"Don't worry about it." She chuckled and waved me away. "He's been waiting to show you what he did in that shed."

"Alright," I said, following Jonahs to the back door.

He pranced down the outside steps and stone path connected to the shed. I was at his heels, observing the mountain peaks and trees.

"Remember how much you used to tease me for keeping bugs hidden in our room?" he asked, opening the shed door.

"Hard to forget finding a whole bunch of crickets in a jar under my bed, Jonahs."

A smirk played on his face as he pulled on a string, turning the lights on and revealing a shelf crowded with fly rods, reels, and nets. He ventured deeper into the shed, coming back with a metal box in hand.

"Look at these!" He dropped the box on a table by the shed's entrance. Inside was a colorful collection of artificial flies.

"Oh, wow." I grabbed one that looked like a moth. "Where did you get these? They look so real."

"I made them." He puffed out his chest. "Been working on them for some time."

"You *made* these?"

"Yes," he said proudly. "All those years reading about and staring at bugs finally amounted to something."

"Ah, I can see it now." I held my hands in the air, holding the shape of an outdoor sign. "Jonahs, God of All Things Creepy and Crawly."

"Very funny." He punched my arm. "And I can see you: Paul, The Stand-Up Comedian Who Failed and Became a Pianist."

"Alright, funny man." My attention returned to the artificial flies. "Do these actually work?"

"They work with me, but we're about to find out if they like you," he replied, turning off the light. "Let's go back inside so I can change."

We returned to the cabin. I sat in the living room while Jonahs went upstairs. It wasn't long until Hannah appeared, taking a seat beside me. "So, how are you?" she asked, her serious face a sight I hadn't seen in a while.

"I'm good." I could tell she wanted my next words to be more than just *How are you?* in response, but I came up short.

Instead, she asked, "How's your ticker?"

"Hasn't given up on me yet." I sighed. "Which is a good thing, I guess."

She laced her fingers over her lap. "He's been alright, by the way," she said, leaning forward to eye the stairs behind me.

"That's good to hear."

Her attention shifted back to me. "Jonahs will be okay. I know you want to ask. Figured I'd save you the time and effort of finding the right moment to do so."

Silence hung for a moment.

"I was scared for him," she continued. "His friends found him wandering in the woods, completely out of himself. When I saw him, his eyes were empty and miles away, staring into nothing. It was as if nobody was home. He kept going on and on about seeing things, visions and such."

"Was he doing any drugs?"

"No, not at all. He smokes a reefer with his college buddies sometimes, but that's not going to trigger a mental breakdown."

My mind raced, searching for the right words, but none were found.

"Today will do him good." She smiled. "He talks about your fishing trips all the time. He needs his older brother. Talk to him." Her eyes glistened. "Sometimes the weight of his program, starting a family, and this whole religion situation—"

Creaks came from the stairs behind the couch, putting an end to our conversation.

"Ready!" Jonahs skipped over the last step, landing on the floor as he zipped up his fly-fishing vest.

"Will you be home for dinner?" Hannah asked as he approached her.

"Probably not." Jonahs bent to kiss her. "Going to take advantage of having this one around. I don't get to go fishing with a famous musician often."

"Okay, Charles Darwin, let's evolve to the truck," I said.

Brothers (part two)

JULY 2005

We loaded our gear into Jonahs' silver truck and got on our way after I grabbed the CD from my car. Whenever he and I were on the road, we'd let the music be our conversation. The melodies and lyrics spoke more than we ever could. I thought about Hannah's words while gazing at the passing scenery. I wanted to ask him what happened, but I wasn't sure how to ease into the subject. There was no easy way to bring it up.

I opened my mouth, determined to ask, but held off when he started singing along to Kris Kristofferson's "Sunday Morning."

On a Sunday morning sidewalk
I'm wishing, Lord, that I was stoned
'Cause there's something in a Sunday
That makes a body feel alone.
And there's nothing short a' dying
That's half as lonesome as the sound
Of the sleeping city sidewalk
And Sunday morning coming down.

We drove about thirty minutes up the canyon road until reaching one of our favorite spots just below the Smith & Morehouse Reservoir. In front of us was the wide dam surrounded by greenery and mountain ranges.

Jonahs and I walked with our fishing gear in hand, dodging the poison ivy bushes. There were plenty of fish in these parts, and the view was something no human could ever get used to.

We put our things down and loaded the pockets of our fishing vests with beef jerky. After grabbing our fly rods, we walked to the edge of the water, its surface so clear I could count every stone at the bottom. Jonahs moved his fly rod back and forth, tossing his artificial fly farther out from the edge of the river. We didn't speak much the first hour. We didn't catch anything either. I glanced at him from the corner of my eye, trying to find a way to break into conversation.

"So, how's the music stuff going?" Jonahs started, keeping his voice down so as not to startle the fish. His words were a relief.

"It's been pretty great," I replied, following his tone. "Had a packed house last week. I'm putting the final touches on *Primary Worship*. Also putting a show together at Kingsbury Hall on September twenty-third. I know it's only July, but I can get you tickets if you'd like."

"Very cool, man." He smiled. "Let me know if you need me

to Photoshop any of your covers again."

I chuckled. "Those were the days. You barely knew how to use—" A fish hit my fly. I stepped into the water, reeling in a beautiful brown trout. "Would you look at that? I guess your flies work!"

"Now that is a beauty," he said.

My attention shifted between the trout and the awestruck expression on his face until we released it back into the water.

"Still jamming with your college band?" I asked as a flock of white-faced ibis crossed our view.

"We get together every once in a while." He reached into his fishing vest pocket and grabbed some beef jerky. "It's fun with the guys."

"That *Vagabond* album was pretty good. Maybe we should've started a band," I said. "The Cardalls."

"That would've been a disaster." He laughed. "I like music, but it's not my life mission. I'm in a good place right now. I've got Hannah and evolutionary biology. I'm set. I'm sure the countless hours studying will pay off at some point. Things are absolutely—" A fish took his fly. He fought with his catch for a few seconds before reeling it in. Another trout, only his was much bigger. He unhooked the fish, its green scales adorned with white scattered dots. Jonahs gazed at the animal as if observing a precious jewel. He carefully bent down and gently released the fish back into the water, as if saying goodbye to a close friend.

"Where was I?" He took a new fly out of his vest and made a quick switch before casting again. "Ah, yes, *Vagabond*. That album was the beginning and end of my music career. By the way, did you have a favorite song off that? I don't think I ever asked."

My eyebrows arched. "The one about Dad's father. I guess we *could* call him Grandpa."

"'The Man I Never Knew,'" he said, casting the fly into the river.

"That one. The lyrics definitely hit home. And props to you for writing a song about the guy who abandoned Dad when he was a kid. That took guts."

"I can't imagine a guy walking out on his family like that. Just disappearing into thin air, never to be heard from again."

"Must've been tough," I agreed. "I also have no idea why a man would walk away from a religion he's served after so many years."

He looked at me, surprised.

"Abandoning your roots can be a dangerous thing," I added. I could tell my sudden comment struck Jonahs like a blow to the stomach. His posture stiffened as he tightened his grip on the rod. But I needed to know if what happened to him was because he had somewhat walked away from his childhood beliefs.

"I don't want to argue," he said in a monotone voice, forcing a smile. "Besides, the fish are listening, and that subject will scare them off."

I shrugged and recast my fly.

"I'm afraid to be happy about this new pregnancy," I confessed, hoping to break the uncomfortable silence that had settled. "It's one thing to hurt for your own life, another to feel the pain of losing someone else, even if unborn. Sometimes it feels as if life is wasting its efforts on a sick man whose clock ticks down faster than others. It's a stupid thought, but…"

"You've always managed to push through. You're still alive even after doctors repeatedly said you'd die. Your boat managed to sail through the storm undamaged."

"The problem is the passengers on my boat get hurt," I said. "Olivia mentioned something before the show last week."

His lips became a rigid line. "What did she say?"

"She revealed that her mom played piano at the Assembly Hall before she got sick." I took in a sharp breath. "She died after that. She seemed to be implying it was my turn now. Not sure what to make of that."

"You think it's regret?" he asked.

"Sometimes I think she's tired of believing we have a long future." I turned to him. "Can you blame her? Maybe her dad was right all along."

Jonahs scoffed, shaking his head. "Come on, who are you kidding? That woman has been in love with you since we were teenagers." His eyes took on a vacant stare. "She wouldn't shut up about you after you guys met. Very few get to live the adventures you do, Paul." He recast his fly. "No matter how dark things get," he added, "you have to look at everything you've survived. Your heart's still beating."

"And my weight fading."

My comment was met with an eyeroll.

"You guys drifted apart after I started dating her," I said. "You used to be such good friends before."

I knew something he thought I didn't; Olivia told me their friendship ended after he gave her a note. She never told me what it said. And he never told me about it. The few times I brought up the note to Olivia, she said it was a private matter.

"People change. Friendships change."

His response was a clear sign I wouldn't get a straight answer from him.

"You're overthinking all of this," he said.

"It wouldn't be the first time." I took a breath before continuing. "I have also been overthinking…you know."

He brought in the line and gently laid his fishing rod on the ground.

"How have you been?" I asked, Sawyer rushing his pace under my chest as a jolt of adrenaline shot down my body.

"Hannah told me you were one of the first ones to show up at the hospital. I still don't know why they had to drive me in an ambulance to a hospital so far away. That bill was a hefty one. I'm thankful you made the drive."

"You gave me quite a scare," I said. "Of course I came."

"Well, thank you." He used the tip of his boot to roll a pebble back and forth on the ground.

"In the ER, you told me what happened. That you were climbing some mountain peak in Idaho, lost your grip, and fell. How you were dangling in the air by your harness with the ground hundreds of feet below. You banged up against the mountain's edge until you finally grabbed hold."

Jonahs watched me reel in my line. "I told you that?" he asked.

"You don't remember?"

"Not really," he said, kicking the pebble to the side. "The whole thing is a blur to me."

"You said you felt strange." A frown carved lines on my forehead. "You went on and on about a voice telling you that your life would be short. Your hair would never gray, and you'd never see your grandchildren."

"I really don't remember." He tucked his hands into his pockets, his attention still on the ground.

"They found you in the woods, Jonahs. I thought you were high."

He took in a sharp breath. "I'm sure many in the family

thought the same thing. Mom and Dad have been hovering over every detail of my life more than ever now."

"Can you blame them? Olivia's pregnancy has really helped me understand our parents. Just look at the life Dad had as a kid. You know he means well and doesn't want your family to go through what he did."

He shuddered at my words. "Have you talked to Dad about your irrational brother yet?"

"Don't say that."

"What?" He shrugged, scrunching his face.

"He's just worried about you, Jonahs."

"I'm sure the whole family thinks this only happened to me because of my declining church attendance." He scoffed. "They probably think I don't believe in God now that I don't attend church." He picked up his rod and cast the fly in the water. "I've heard Dad say that as long as you're doing what's right in the eyes of God, your life will be preserved. What's that about?" He grabbed another beef jerky from his pocket. "Different people have different perceptions of God. They find God in different ways. There are countless surgeons who aren't religious and operate miracles on people every day."

Sadness flooded his eyes and his breathing grew heavy.

"Are you alright?" I asked.

"Look, I don't know what came over me during that climb.

I lost control, but I was conscious, if that makes sense. And all I want is a moment of relief where I don't feel like I'm living for the world around me, or church, or for Mom and Dad. I want to live for myself."

"Are you thinking about seeking more help?"

"They had me see a therapist at the hospital." He scratched his buzzed head. "I'm not sure, to be honest. I feel fine now. Anyway—whoa!" There was a strong pull on his rod. He reeled in his line, a thrashing trout at the end.

"Notice how the flies shaped like caddis catch bigger fish?" He unhooked the trout, the sadness of his eyes long gone. "This one is a beauty."

"So you're okay?" I asked, checking one more time before I let him change the subject.

His eyes rolled. "Yes, Paul. I. Am. Okay."

He released the fish back into the water.

Jonahs' artificial flies worked miracles the rest of the afternoon. Streaks of orange and purple painted the sky as the sun set behind the mountains. I insisted on leaving before nightfall, but Jonahs was determined to stay.

By the time we left the river and returned to the truck, a few scattered stars had appeared. We sat on the tailgate as the sun waved the day goodbye.

As soon as dusk settled, Jonahs rushed to the driver side door.

"What are you doing?" I shouted, legs dangling, a cold can of Diet Coke in hand.

The only response was the blaring sound of Rush's "Tom Sawyer" echoing across the canyon.

He jumped back on the truck's tailgate. "You're welcome!" He shoved my shoulder forward while singing. "*A modern-day warrior, Mean mean stride*'—Come on. Sing with me."

"*Today's Tom Sawyer, Mean mean pride*,'" I rushed the lyrics to catch up with the melody.

A duet ensued. He grabbed a water bottle from the cooler and held it like a microphone, swaying his hand to the song.

"*Today's Tom Sawyer, He gets high on you, And the space he invades, He gets by on you.*'"

I waved at Jonahs. "Can you lower the volume?"

"*No, his mind is not for rent*'—"

"Hey!"

"What, Paul? This is the best part!" he shouted.

"Lower the volume!" I repeated.

He did as I requested, coming back with slumped shoulders and a pout. "Dang, you can kill a mood." He sat on the edge of the tailgate, arms crossed over his chest.

"There's this secret I've never told anyone. Not even Olivia." I slouched forward, elbows on my knees.

"Now I'm interested."

"I named my heart Tom Sawyer," I whispered.

"Are you serious?" His eyes widened, hands spread in the air. "You followed my advice all those years ago?"

"I did. And it's helped me deal with him."

"How come you never told anyone?" he asked.

"Feels good having a secret broken friend. Anyway, thought I'd tell you."

"I will carry this secret to my grave," he said solemnly, hand on his chest and head bowed.

We both laughed.

My gaze turned upward. "Would you look at that? So many stars."

"No light pollution." He pointed to one of the constellations. "There's the Big Dipper. If you're ever lost, that star will always point north. It's visible all year long."

"Shame it can't guide me to a healthy heart."

"Yeah," he mumbled. "Shame."

"Do you actually believe in God, though?" The look he gave me signaled that I had just ruined the moment. "I'm not talking about church. Just asking because you said you believe in God. And you're right, some in the family question it. But with so many unanswered questions, different religious systems, and all the scientific facts—how do you know there's a higher power out there?"

"Can't you feel it?" he asked as if it was obvious.

"Feel what?"

"For a moment, forget the do's and the don'ts. Forget the how's and the where's. Let go of all the rules and regulations we were taught." His gaze shifted back to the stars. "Just look up at the sky again."

I did as he requested, even though I didn't really agree with his statement; the do's and don'ts pointed us to the truth.

"Can't you *feel* it?" His voice echoed in my ears. "God was there before we used religion and politics to control things. He created each of us to be different and saw that it was good. I don't believe God wants everyone in the same belief system. He has a different adventure for every single one of us. And yet, there's so much shaming toward people like me who simply want to investigate the beauty beyond the things I already know."

"What do you feel?" I asked.

"I'm like a moth surrounded by butterflies; harmless, but I still seem like a threat. The misfit will always be judged until understood."

Jonahs got off the back of the truck, walked to one of the pine trees, plucked a pinecone, and came back. "While some go into a building made of dead trees to have a spiritual experience, I come here where the trees are alive." He smiled and stabbed a finger at the pinecone. "Church definitely doesn't smell like this."

I leaned closer and inhaled the pine scent. "No, it doesn't.

But I can pack some for the next time you decide to go to church." He tossed the pinecone on the ground, a defeated expression on his face. "Sounds like you're just challenging tradition," I added as he sat beside me.

"I'm just trying to balance my pursuit of truth as both a scientist and believer of a higher power. Galileo was accused of heresy by the church when he suggested the Earth wasn't the center of the universe. He had the scientific facts, but theologians decided it was the other way around. According to them, the sun revolving around the Earth was an undisputed fact of scripture. Maybe they were just upset the information came from a scientist and not one of them first."

"Interesting," I mumbled.

"You know what else is funny?" He leaned closer. "If Galileo was alive today, his hypothesis might go something like: *The Earth is no longer the center of the universe. People are.*"

"No lie there."

"Galileo's truth made him guilty in the eyes of religion. They banned his book and stopped him from teaching. He spent the rest of his life under house arrest. Three hundred years later, the Vatican admits the guy was right all along." He scoffed and shook his head. "I'm willing to take the fall for the truth I discover in this life even if people only understand it after I'm long gone."

"I admire you." My words triggered a broad smile on his face. "Your determination to discover something new is what many wished they had. I just hope you have the same determination to understand the truth that's already in front of you."

His lips became a rigid line again. He startled me when he suddenly rushed toward the back door, grabbing an old acoustic guitar tucked up against the back window.

"What else do you have in there?" I asked as he approached.

"The doorway to Narnia." He sat back on the tailgate and began tuning the strings.

He played a melody I knew far too well. "How Great Thou Art" was one of the songs they played almost every time I attended church. It meant so much to me, I ended up recording a rendition of it.

His fingers fiddled with the strings. The stars held his gaze. He'd strike a wrong chord here and there. I could tell he was rusty, which probably meant he wasn't really playing music with his friends after all. Or maybe he was just rusty when it came to playing hymns. I wondered what else he kept hidden. What other things did he bottle up inside? Maybe what he called a pursuit was actually an attempt to run away from something.

Jonahs was only twenty-nine, but he had wisdom far beyond his years; his words whirled in my head like the wrong notes he struck while playing the song. There was truth to them, but they were out of order, muddled together by a spark of rebellion. I wanted to question more of his comments, but unlike him, I could keep my own rebellion at bay.

THE MAN I NEVER KNEW

They say he was a handsome man,
slight of build and not too tall.
Full of charm and charisma,
he easily had the attention of all.
At twenty-one, he met himself a lady.
Soon he made that lady his wife.
But war broke out in a foreign land,
he had to leave his newly wed behind.

He became a traveling soldier.
Fought for his country in World War II.
He became a traveling soldier.
He's the man I never knew.

Well peace came,
he returned to the valley
finally to settle down with his bride.
Bur perhaps what he did
in those South Pacific seas
wouldn't let the man sleep at night.

Well five children later
and growing discontent.
He was waiting for his ship to come in.
He started hitting the bottle too hard
as he turned to a lifetime of sin.

He became a traveling merchant.
His wife and children
didn't know what to do.
He became a traveling merchant.
He's the man I never knew.

Roaming around this great country,
the days of Denver
with Jack Kerouac on the road.
Could he have been in New York City
when Bob Dylan was singing
"Pretty Peggy-O"?
Well times got hard. He hit the bottle.
Then the bottle took over his life
with unpaid bills and disappointment.
Then the love he lost
when he cheated on his wife.

He became a traveling hobo
to phoenix town the rails he rode.
He became a traveling hobo.
He's the man I'll never know.

Well out on the streets,
he lived as a drunkard.
He was still waiting for his ship to come in.
And often times he would sit and dream,
"Where are those five pretty children?"

There were forty empty bottles
scattered all around.
The dirty mattress
where he'd lay on his side.
Alone there in his woe and petty,
that poor lost soul quietly died.

So tell me, dear granddaddy.
Where is it now you're traveling to?
Tell me, dear granddaddy.
'Cause you're the man I never knew.

Tell me, dear granddaddy.

Where is it now you're traveling to?

Did you make it into heaven or get sent down below?

You're the man I never knew.

You're the man I never knew.

Tom Sawyer

JULY 1986

Laughter echoed around the house as everyone got ready for dinner. Dad wanted us all at the table to celebrate, well, me. I'd finally completed all of the requirements and earned enough merit badges to be an Eagle Scout. As part of the celebration, Mom made enough food for an entire battalion; I asked if I could invite a couple of friends from school, but she told me dinner that night was for family only.

There was a knock on my bedroom door. Which was, in fact, a room located in the basement, shared by me and my brothers, Dan and Jonahs.

"Come in," I said.

"Hurry up." Jonahs walked in and sat on his bed, wearing a blue button-down and khaki pants. Mom had probably tried combing his hair, but he had this thing where he never wanted his hair to look too polished, so he'd run his hand through it, making it look like a dark bird's nest.

"Liking the hair," I said, looking at mine in the mirror

hanging on the wall, making sure all strands were still glued in place by some cheap hair gel.

"Don't be jealous of my looks."

Sharing a bedroom with my brothers assured me of a couple of things: a) We'd never go to bed on time, b) It was their right to barge in on me whenever they felt like it, and c) Due to their annoying behavior, a fight was bound to happen at any moment.

But sharing a room with Jonahs came with other side effects. I'd sometimes find bugs hidden under my bed or in my closet; he had a habit of trapping them inside glass jars and keeping them around without telling anyone. The one time he captured a cricket, none of us slept a wink.

"I can't even get dressed in peace," I said. "And I still don't understand why it took everyone longer to get ready for a dinner party happening at our own house than it does to go to church on Sunday. Seriously."

"You're the special sibling." Jonahs lay on his side. "The Eagle Scout with a broken heart."

"Very funny."

Jonahs sat up on the bed, looking as if he had discovered a treasure. "You should name it!"

"Name what?" My brows pulled together.

"Your heart. If I had a heart like yours, I'd look at it as a messed-up friend or a wounded hero." He pursed his lips. "Every broken hero needs an epic name."

"You think my messed-up heart is a hero?"

"It's keeping you alive."

I buttoned up my shirt in silence.

"I'd name mine after a character," he continued. "Or a song!"

"I think that's your ten-year-old-head talking, buddy." I took a step back from the mirror, checking myself one last time. "Maybe you could name yours after a bug. You love those."

"Say what you want. I think it's a great idea." He leapt to his feet and walked to the door. "See you at the table. Everyone is waiting upstairs."

After he closed the door behind him, I spotted my copy of *Huckleberry Finn* on the floor by my bed. The edges of the cover were torn and the spine bent from all the hours spent reading it. The sight sparked fond memories of my favorite character and song, "Tom Sawyer."

With a hand over my heart, I said, "Sawyer…Sawyer…"

Everyone was gathered around the table, their chatter turning to unrehearsed claps once I walked into the dining room. My older siblings, Kirsten and Carla, stood to their feet, clearly cheering me on only because Mom and Dad had asked them to. I called them The Unrelated Twins since, despite being born on the same day, they looked nothing alike. My older sister, Molly, sat beside them. Jonahs tapped the empty chair beside him.

"Proud of you, Paul," said Dan as I took a seat next to Jonahs. "You've got your Eagle, but remember, I was the first to learn how to swim *and* jump off a diving board. You have some catching up to do." He was my younger brother, though still older than Jonahs. "But look at you." He nudged me with an elbow. "Becoming a family legend already."

"Yes, Dan," I said in an English accent, my fingers laced over the table as if I attended some fancy dinner party. "I'm aware you're Superman."

"It'll do you good to remember that."

Janice and Greg, who were eight and three, looked at us like we were cartoon characters.

"Alright, alright. That's enough." Dad was up on his feet, hands spread out. "Let's settle down. I know we're all hungry." Everyone fell silent. His eyes bore into mine. "But before we eat, I'd like to honor Paul for this incredible achievement. I'm extremely proud, Son. Very few young men are ever able to get the Eagle Scout rank." He choked up.

I immediately knew who he meant. Dad told me he was a scout leader, but due to life's unexpected surprises, he never got the Eagle. He didn't speak of his childhood or teenage years much, his parents' divorce a painful memory to this very day.

"And to get an Eagle Scout award at thirteen…" He continued after finding his voice again, "So proud."

My eyes scanned the faces of everyone around me, eventually landing on Jonahs. He rested his forehead on the edge of the table face down beside me. He seemed to be examining something.

"What are you doing?" I whispered.

"Just looking at something," he said softly, still in the same position.

"Mom, will you pray and thank our Father in Heaven for His love and support?" Dad asked.

Everyone folded their arms on their laps and closed their eyes, listening to Mom pray. My eyes were half open during the prayer. Jonahs held his position until she was done.

"Dude, are you alright?" I asked, trying to peek at whatever held his attention while the others went for the food.

Mom approached Jonahs and rested a hand on his shoulder.

"What do you have there?" she asked.

He quickly lifted his head. "It's a secret."

Mom bent down, meeting his gaze. "You can tell me."

Jonahs' hands were cupped together. He beckoned Mom closer with a nod. She leaned in, curious. He whispered something in her ear, earning a few giggles from her. They looked alike. They had the same hazel eyes and chiseled chin. Jonahs opened his cupped hands, and I spotted the fluttering wings of a gray moth in his grasp. But one of them was broken.

"Their wings don't heal," Jonahs whimpered. "I know it looks scary, but moths aren't bad." He pouted his lips. "Can I keep it in my room?"

I shook my head at Mom. I had enough jars with bugs under my bed as it was.

"Sweetheart, you can't," Mom whispered. "It'll die inside a jar."

"But it'll also die out there," he retorted.

"Wouldn't it be better for it to die in its home rather than ours?" Mom smiled.

"Okay." Jonahs' eyes welled up.

"Want me to set it free through the back door, honey?"

Jonahs handed her the wounded moth like it was a baby. Mom retreated to the kitchen, opened the back door, and then returned to the table. She wiped her hand on her apron, a bottle of salad dressing in the other.

Dad asked where she went, and she simply shook the bottle in the air, sending Jonahs a wink.

"How did you get a moth in here?" I asked him.

"I didn't get it in here, genius. It was on the leg of my chair, but I had to get it out before anyone saw it. Kirsten would've flipped out."

"Like she did with the cricket?" I grinned.

"It was just that one time," he said.

Different subjects came up as we ate; the majority of them being about my achievement. It felt good to have my family celebrate something I thought was impossible for me to do. I listened and chimed in, but watching Jonahs build a dam out of his mashed potatoes was far more entertaining. He was completely engrossed in the act, even building a river with his gravy and planting trees out of broccoli.

Mom and Dad tried to get him involved in the conversation, but no subject was interesting enough to hold his attention for long. He was too busy creating a new world.

Darkness

JULY 1986

I woke up the day after the celebration dinner to find the other empty beds still messy. That meant Mom was waiting for me to wake up so she could help me tidy the room.

My room had three beds: on the left was Dan's, the one in the middle Jonahs', and mine was on the far right. Though the room was in the basement, the window beside my bed provided a bit of sunlight, which was something I enjoyed waking up to in the mornings.

I lay in bed for a while, replaying the previous night's dinner in my head, hands folded over my chest. Sawyer clipped along at a jog as the memories filled my mind: Dad's proud face, Mom's eyes staring at me like I was a hero, and Jonahs making his mashed potato dams.

After being lazy for a few more minutes, I jumped up, only to have the room spin around me. For a few moments, I was on a merry-go-round without any handholds. I stood rooted to the spot, arms spread out. One of my hands jolted to my chest. Sawyer's beating felt different, like a drummer who'd lost their groove.

I took a step forward when my surroundings settled. Nothing moved.

"Guess I'm just hungry," I said, though Sawyer still felt strange.

I walked out of my bedroom and saw the other two rooms were empty, beds already made. I entered the bathroom and glanced at the clock on the wall.

"Eleven fifteen!" I barked.

I enjoyed sleeping in every once in a while but never this late. Dad always told us that a day was wasted if someone slept past ten. I took a shower, brushed my teeth, and changed in less than twenty minutes.

Sawyer fluttered as I walked upstairs, leaving me light-headed. I halted halfway, pressing my back against the wall. Ragged breaths followed as everything spun again. It felt like the distance between me and the doorway was hundreds of miles long. If I passed out, my body would roll down the stairs like a bowling ball. I pressed my eyes shut and attempted to control my breathing.

A minute passed and the room no longer spun when I chanced a look. Sawyer calmed, beating evenly. I took a step up, holding on to the rail as if my life depended on it—which, at the moment, it did.

"You're awake!" Mom said, appearing at the top of the stairs. "I was about to come get you up. I need you to clean that basement before it's destroyed by your siblings again. It's your week after all. Dad has everyone else weeding the flower beds outside."

"Well...hi, Mom." I forced a smile, hoping to conceal my fear. I didn't want to alarm anyone.

"Are you alright?" she asked, hands on her waist. "You're pale."

"Yeah, just hungry." I managed to make my way into the kitchen.

"Are you sure?" she insisted.

"I'm fine. Kind of upset I lost the whole day." I frowned. "Why did you let me sleep in?"

She stared into my eyes like she had some sort of super-power that could scan my brain for the truth. "Go eat," she said. "There's still some food left."

I was fine.

Sawyer was fine.

I was just hungry.

I sat on one of the stools by the counter. There was bread, scrambled eggs, juice, and milk.

Once I fixed myself a plate, I moved to the red couch by the window and sat on its arm so I could admire the view. Mount Olympus was on full display. Climbing to the top had been a dream of mine for as long as I could remember, but I knew the possibility of that happening was slim. Sawyer would never let me, and unless I got a brand-new heart, Mount Olympus' summit would remain a fruit of my imagination. That's the thing about living with half a heart—you get used to the things you want remaining dreams. Nothing more.

A couple of my friends came by in the afternoon and invited me to play football with them and some other guys. The game was kind of perfect for someone in my condition since players had to stop constantly. It allowed me to catch my breath and for Sawyer to build up his strength.

I marched down the stairs into the basement and retreated to my room to change. Images of my almost-fainting-on-the-stairs incident spooked me as I got dressed. I brushed it off. It was nothing to worry about. I had been fine since then.

"I'm alright," I said to myself. "Sawyer's alright."

The field was a short five-minute walk from the house. The conversation ranged from cute girls to their excitement about waving Evergreen Middle School goodbye to say hello to Mount Olympus High in the fall. Sure, I was going to miss them, but I'd be joining them in a year.

The game started a few minutes after we arrived. All the other kids were from Park Middle School across town. Apparently, this was the only open field available. Understandable, since people in Salt Lake were intense about their summers.

I was reluctant during the first few moments of the game, still taking it easy on Sawyer. I brushed off my concern after a few touchdowns. But then I got worse; my entire body went cold and numb. I squinted my eyes, trying to remain focused on the field, but everything blurred. Sawyer lost his groove. I put my trembling hands on my knees, bent down, and squeezed my eyes shut. It was happening again, only this time in front of friends and strangers. I gasped for air, but my lungs failed to breathe.

Darkness.

There was this constant, annoying beeping sound in my head. I thought it was a dream until my eyes fluttered open.

I didn't recognize the wallpaper. It was blue and crowded with pictures of farm animals. There was a window to my right with salmon curtains, the sky outside dark, the lights of the city a bright display. I felt an itch on my cheek while searching for the source of all the beeping. There was a tug on my hand as I raised it, and I shuddered at the sight of the IV in my vein. Then I noticed the turquoise gown.

"Paul?" My face turned toward the familiar voice. Mom sat on a brown leather chair, a book on her lap. She gave me a trembling smile. "Oh, thank goodness you're awake."

She shifted from the leather chair to the edge of the bed.

"What happened?" I asked, trying to recall how I ended up at the hospital.

"What's the last thing you remember?"

"I was playing ball." My words turned to ragged breaths. "And then I...I was..."

"You passed out in the middle of the game." Her chin wobbled. "They called your father at work and told him you were being brought here. They're doing some tests to see what's going on."

"Where's Dad?"

"He went to the cafeteria to get us some decent food." A teary smile found her face. "At least you're awake. I was so scared, honey. I'm going to call the nurse. I'm sure she'll want to talk to you."

My eyes followed her until she closed the door.

Anger wrapped itself around me. I fainted in front of all those people. My tears wanted to escape, but I fought against them. I guess I thought life was willing to skip this chapter and let me go on as if Sawyer was okay. But I was a fool with a messed-up heart. I thought winning all those merit badges meant I could have somewhat of a normal life, but being here—where they do nothing but fix broken people—was a reminder. In the same way climbing Mount Olympus would remain a dream, a healthy Sawyer would be nothing but desire.

Mom returned with a nurse—a very cute one at least. She had blonde hair and bright blue eyes matching the stripes on her white scrubs.

"Hey there, Paul. My name is Christie." She smiled. "Happy to see you're awake! I need to ask you a few things."

A flood of questions began. I felt like a celebrity being interviewed—only she was interested in my disease and health, not my charm. She wrote on her notepad with great determination. Mom struggled to keep a straight face as she listened.

"I think I have all I need," Christie said. "I'm going to speak to the doctor. Meanwhile, don't eat any solid food until we have more updates. Do call if you need anything."

Dad emerged holding a tray of food as soon as she walked out, the smell of chicken filling the entire room.

"Hey, Dad," I said, dry-mouthed from all the interview questions.

"You're awake!" He rushed inside, setting the tray on a table by the bed. There were mashed potatoes with gravy and applesauce. "Is everything okay? Any updates?"

"We'll know soon," Mom replied.

"Good, good." Dad's eyes grew vacant. "Meanwhile, let's eat."

"Let's play a game," I said with a smirk, trying to break the tension. "Let's see how long it's going to take me to vomit up this hospital food."

Mom scrunched her face. "That sounds fun."

"Then give me the chicken."

"You better stick to applesauce for now," Dad said.

"Might as well not eat then." I shrugged. "Mushy food."

"Here, Paul." He opened the plastic cup and handed it to me with a spoon. "You need to have something in your system."

We ate in silence.

I knew they hurt for me.

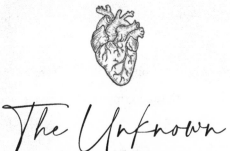

The Unknown

NOVEMBER 2005

"I'll get it!" I shouted, grabbing the yellow baby bag from the counter. Olivia stood by the door wearing a brown coat, hand on her enormous belly. It was time. Her contractions started after coming home from her shift early in the afternoon. By six p.m., they averaged eight minutes apart, a clear sign Neil was coming.

"The contractions could've started while I was still at work. It would've saved us a car ride to the hospital during rush hour," she said, buttoning up her coat and opening the door, a cold November wind greeting us.

"Sweetie, if only there was an alarm clock for these things," I said, helping her down the stairs of the porch and into the car. Sawyer was in a frenzy, as excited as I was about seeing Neil's face for the first time.

Rush's "Closer to the Heart" started playing the moment I started the car.

"Of course this would be the soundtrack of our hospital

trip." She smiled with a nod. "I guess Neil is meant to love Rush, too."

"We're about to go on the wildest adventure of our lives," I said, my knuckles white from gripping the steering wheel so hard. "We need iconic music for the ride. By the way, you did pay attention to those birthing classes, right?"

"As much as you did."

"Then we're in trouble!"

"Very funny," she said.

Mount Olympus stared at me as we drove, the sky painted in streaks of orange and dark blue.

"Paul, slow down!" Olivia latched onto the grab handle after I drove over a hill. "Pregnant women don't ride roller coasters. And try not to get us pulled over."

"Sorry, sorry. Just excited. We're about to do this!"

I swerved and cut through every car in traffic like I was in a game of *Pole Position*. A couple of middle fingers and horns were sent my way in retribution.

Once at the hospital, we were told by Dr. Homer that Olivia was dilated one centimeter and had to stay overnight. She was dilated three centimeters by midnight.

Olivia was ready to push at one p.m. the next day. The nurse and I guided her through the first series of pushes until Dr. Homer arrived. Sawyer leaped wildly under my ribcage. My fingers tingled as if playing a new melody on the piano.

The world stopped when I spotted a small patch of brown hair as he made his way into our world. The doctor pulled him from Olivia, handing him to the nurse. She held him up and spanked his bottom. Neil's cry was the most powerful melody to have ever graced my ears. No song I had written or melody I ever composed could compare to its sound. The nurse approached me with a smile, my son in her arms. I followed them to a table where I was given a cloth to clean him up.

"Hey, little Neil." The wisps of dark hair on his reddish scalp remained visible despite my welling tears. "I'm your dad and you're my son." His cheeks were round and puffy, his hands small. "We're going to be best buddies."

"Wrap him with this," said the nurse, handing me a white blanket.

Neil ceased his crying after I wrapped him.

He smacked his lips and cooed as I laid him in Olivia's arms. We gazed upon our son. After two painful miscarriages, here we were, witnessing a living miracle.

Sawyer had never beaten with such determination. It was my heart's constant thumping and my son's face that sent a shiver down my spine. I had wanted this for so long that my own limitations slipped my mind.

The weeks that followed Neil's arrival were an adventure. Sleeping a whole night became a ridiculous notion. Our new pastimes became diaper changing, sleep-rocking, and making sure the water in his tub wasn't scorching hot. It was the best worst thing to ever happen to us, and we wouldn't trade it for the world. Olivia's smile gave me hope she could see past the unknowns and beyond the *what ifs*. Maybe finally having a child of our own was what she needed.

When Neil came home, I hung the mobile above the white crib and spun it to make sure it worked. But the sound of the innocent lullaby brought a sense of impending doom. I saw the spinning plastic animals and thought of a possible future where I wouldn't get to see the crib replaced with a bed.

The image of my son asleep in his crib did push away some of those thoughts. But they lingered, hovering like vultures over a carcass. In his innocent face, I saw some of my mom. She told me that when I was a newborn, she didn't even want to sleep in a separate room. *Is his heart pumping? Is he breathing? Is he alive? Am I going to wake up to find him dead?* I never understood or fully appreciated the love my parents had for me until Neil.

After his birth, any free time I had was spent at my piano.

We had placed his room upstairs so the music wouldn't wake him. Inspiration was more constant than ever. Songs of gratitude, hope, and faith flowed out of me. One particular melody whirled in my head relentlessly, especially when he was near me. During one of my almost-nonexistent free times, I composed a song called "Our Love"—a dedication to my own little piece of paradise.

I was at the piano working on the piece, repeating the opening again and again when the phone suddenly interrupted me. I rushed to the living room, annoyed as to who dared disturb my creative escape, not to mention Olivia and Neil's nap. I looked at the caller ID. It was Walter, my booking agent.

"Paul, I may have a gig for you this time." The sound of his smoke-damaged voice sent a heatwave down my body.

"Well, hey, I'm great. Olivia and Neil are fantastic," I retorted. "I thought you knew I was taking the month off to be with them."

"And I heard you, but my job is to help you get gigs. That's what you wanted me to do, right?"

That's what I wanted him to do, but he barely did it. He had me spend thousands on printed ads and conferences in the hope presenters would book me. His ideas always meant he would sit back, and I had to do the legwork.

"I'm telling you, Paul." A nervous laugh escaped him. "This one is big."

"Just spill it," I said, wondering why I didn't have it in me to let this guy go.

"I got this opportunity to have you do a series of Christmas concerts in the upper Midwest. Good money. Good exposure. Bigger venue. It's a nice way to keep momentum going for your new album. I figured this could also be a good fit since you did that Christmas record in 2003. I'm forwarding you the email from the Arts Council with all the details. You'll like the offer."

I retreated upstairs to my office, phone in hand. To my surprise, Walter wasn't lying. The gig paid well and presented the opportunity to introduce my music to thousands of people who had never heard it before.

"Are you in?" he asked.

I knew the right thing to do was consult Olivia, but my mouth spoke faster than my mind. "Sounds great."

"Fantastic. And you can put a band and set together by December sixteenth, right?"

"Sure," I mumbled, my mind scurrying for a solution to his request.

"Great! It's settled. Can't wait to see you then."

Creaks echoed from the hall. Olivia appeared, face puffed, hair tied into a bun. She wore a long white shirt and pajama bottoms.

"Slept okay?" I asked.

"I never thought I'd treasure sleep that much." She smiled. "Come to the kitchen. I need water."

The two of us headed downstairs.

"Who was that on the phone?" She walked to the cabinet and grabbed a glass.

"Walter," I said, resting my shoulder on the wall, arms folded over my chest.

She tensed, holding the glass under the water filter on the fridge. "What did he want? I know he wasn't calling to congratulate you. I still don't know why you put up with that guy. Aren't agents supposed to book actual gigs?"

"You're funny." I smirked.

How was I going to break the news to her?

"Everything okay?" Olivia asked.

"There's an opportunity for me to play a couple of Christmas concerts next month."

She scoffed and set the glass on the counter, hands on her waist. "But Thanksgiving is this Thursday." A frown appeared on her face. "That would put an incredible weight on us right now. What did you tell him?"

My lips pressed into a line. "That I was going to do it. It's the first thing he's gotten me in months. It pays well."

Her cheeks flushed. "How do you think you're going to accomplish that?"

"I'll find a way. I'll get some people together, get a band going. We need the money. When you go back to the hospital it's only going to be part-time. And I need to keep the momentum going on this new album. He forwarded me the email from the Arts Council. They want me to be part of it."

"Did you even think about us?"

"I'll be gone for four, five days tops. And you're both the reason why I'm doing this."

"Of course we are," she said snidely. "Maybe shows just aren't for us. Walter keeps struggling to get you booked for these types of things. Maybe it's a sign"

"Remember when you told me living off album sales alone wasn't a reality? Look at us now. My *Hymns* records have been our bread and butter. I wish I could spend every single moment with the both of you, but—"

"My uncle had the same mindset." Her arms flailed. "Let me go out and tour and make my music known. That will bring the family money. Look how that turned out. And then there was my cousin—"

"My music has been putting actual food on the table."

"I'm not denying that. I just feel you need something more sustainable for your health now that we have a son," she said.

"Gigs like these are sustainable. Our family needs this right now."

She pursed her lips. "Why didn't you ask me what I thought?"

Silence.

Life Can Be Mean

AUGUST 1986

I had been in the hospital for almost a month since I passed out on the field. I kept getting skinnier by the day, and things got boring quickly while I was cooped up in there. Despite the new MRI scans, none of my cardiologists could find the source of the infection killing me. Whenever I went inside that machine, I thought of a mad scientist about to terminate one of his subjects.

I was always tired. Always sleeping. Always weak. At least I got to watch a lot of meaningless television from bed. When *The Price is Right* becomes a morning routine, you're either retired or—like me—in the hospital.

Cute nurse Christie and I became pals. She was my outlet for good conversation.

I was convinced the hospital wanted to kick my family out when the siblings came to visit. Things got loud really fast.

On a day when my parents were visiting with Jonahs, one of the doctors came into the room with a folder and clipboard in hand. He was probably lingering outside the hall waiting for an adult to show up before entering.

"Mr. and Mrs. Cardall, my name is Dr. Donald," he said, clearly forcing a smile.

"Pleasure," Mom said with a look of concern.

"And who's this guy?" He bent down, meeting Jonahs at eye level.

"Jonahs," he said, coiling into himself.

"Nice to meet you." His attention shifted to my parents. "Could we talk in private?"

"You have news?" There was a hint of worry in Mom's voice.

"Maybe we should talk outside." Dr. Donald seemed hesitant.

"You know I can hear everything you guys say on the other side of those walls, right?" I asked. "I can take it. It's my heart after all."

Everyone in the room gave me a look of surprise.

"Go ahead, Doctor," Dad said after a brief silence.

"Alright." Dr. Donald sat down on one of the chairs lined up against the wall, my parents beside him. He glanced at me as if I was a ghost, filled his chest with air, and started, "We found the cause of his problem on the last MRI." Sawyer went for a jog as the doctor opened the folder in his hand, revealing a paper crowded with black and white photos of my heart. One of them was circled, with an arrow pointing to a white dot in the upper left corner. "See this?" He tapped the dot with a finger. "This is a viral infection on the section of the heart where he was operated on as a baby. It's as big as a walnut and has to be removed as soon as possible."

"Is it a risky procedure?" There was a hitch in Dad's voice.

Dr. Donald's attention shifted between my parents and me. "Maybe it's best—"

"Just say it!" I barked, body flushed with anger and fear.

"It's life-threatening." My parents' faces paled. "There's a real chance he might not survive the surgery."

I was shocked. Frozen.

"Any chance this diagnosis could be wrong?" Dad leaned forward, elbows on his knees.

"We'll be taking a look at the heart during surgery to make sure nothing else is damaged," Dr. Donald replied, his right leg bouncing up and down. "But as of right now, this is the diagnosis. I'm sorry it isn't better news."

"When are you planning on doing the surgery?" Mom asked.

"Early in the morning. We can't wait much longer. I apologize it took so long to find the infection, but now that we did, we can't waste time."

Jonahs stared at Dr. Donald as if he was a monster. The frown on his face carved wrinkles so deep, they could pass for chasms. Jonahs might have been ten, but if his eyes could fight, they would've destroyed the doctor on the spot.

Dr. Donald stood with a silent nod and walked out of the room.

"At least they found it," I said weakly.

"You'll be fine, sweetie." Mom sat on the edge of my bed and grabbed my hand. "Everything will be okay."

"I guess it's time to add another scar to my collection, only this time right on my chest."

Jonahs walked to the other side of the bed, jumped up, and lay down beside me. "At least you'll look even more dangerous without a shirt."

The four of us shared a brief laugh.

I wasn't sure how hard they tried to conceal their shock and fear. Honestly, no human being was capable of masking their feelings when receiving news like this. Funny enough, I didn't fear death. Cute nurse Christie said the kids are always less afraid than their parents.

But I did fear how my death would affect the ones who loved me.

Jonahs stayed on the bed as my parents left the room to make a call. We didn't speak. We watched cartoons and enjoyed each other's company. He'd glance up and stare at me like I was some bionic being with superpowers.

My parents returned to the room.

"Dad's going to go pick up your siblings so they can come see you before the surgery." Mom sat in the brown leather chair beside my bed. Dad stood still, hands in his jean pockets.

"I *will* make it," I said, my voice catching in my throat.

"Of course you will." Tears welled in Dad's eyes. "I have no doubt about it."

Once he left, Jonahs and I continued watching television while Mom read her book. She loved to read and, even at her darkest, a book was the light that made her smile.

An unusual silence lingered when my siblings arrived. Whenever we were together, laughter, jokes, and fights would follow. Not that day. I tried to keep a straight face so they wouldn't notice how weak I was, how much fear gripped me, and how much I didn't want to disappoint them by leaving this world.

I fell asleep that night thinking about life, death, my family, and Sawyer. A part of me was relieved they found the little monster attacking Sawyer, and then there was the part that really didn't want to die.

I woke up to the blurry sight of my parents sitting by my bed. My surroundings spun as if I was on a merry-go-round. The wallpaper was different from my previous room, the farm animals replaced with flowers.

"Paul?" Even as the room spun, Mom's pink blouse was something I couldn't miss. "Paul, you're awake!"

"Am I in heaven?" I mumbled. "Because if I am, I'm requesting they take down this wallpaper."

"How are you feeling?" Dad's voice was a distant, muffled sound. "Paul?"

Everything went dark.

When I opened my eyes again, Mom was the only one in the room; she wore a blouse with polka dots, eyes on the television, legs crossed.

I felt something lodged in my throat. It wasn't long until I realized there was a tube coming out of my mouth. My attention shifted to my exposed chest. Four tubes flowed out of my ribcage, draining fluid from my lungs into a box placed on the right side of the bed. The fresh wound overlaid my sternum, sewn shut by many sutures.

My hand curled into a fist at the pain. I managed to let out a groan.

She jumped up from the chair. "Paul!" She lowered the volume using the remote. "You're okay."

Her glistening eyes locked on mine. The breath in my lungs, Sawyer beating away under my chest, the pain, and my mom's face meant that I was alive. I made it. I survived.

The tube in my trachea made it impossible to get a word out. "You're in the ICU," Mom said, knowing what I wanted to ask. "They want to keep you here for a while to make sure you're okay." She swallowed her words, pressing her lips into a line. "But of course you're okay. You're here."

The days that followed were a struggle to bear. From doctors switching the tubes out after draining fluids out of my body to the anxiety of not knowing what would happen next. The pain and the situation exhausted me.

I questioned my reasons for staying alive. I knew my death would hurt those who loved me, but clinging to life turned into a pain of its own.

I was eventually moved out of the ICU, but doctors and nurses kept a close watch the whole time. I felt claustrophobic, suffocated, useless—and somewhat of a disappointment despite surviving the procedure. Sawyer and I were to blame for this mess. To add even more excitement to my teenage years, Dr. Donald broke the news that I'd need reconstructive heart surgery within a year.

I couldn't bear the thought of doctors prying me open again. The possibility this would become my life made me question why I even wanted to live in the first place. What was the point of living a life like this?

To everyone's surprise, I went home after a week of recovery. Despite my body managing to heal faster than anticipated, I was going to be homeschooled for a few weeks. Dr. Donald wanted to ensure my wounds were fully healed before I returned to school.

Mom was assigned the task of being my private teacher. Because that's what everyone going into eighth grade dreams of, their mom being their teacher. I loved my parents, but school was my excuse to catch a break from family.

As the days went on, I realized classes with her weren't so bad after all. We would have breakfast together every day, and she'd cook lunch. I'd always finish my studies early so I could have some extra free time, which I looked at as a reward for having survived open-heart surgery.

Jonahs and Dan kept an extra close watch during those weeks of recovery. They'd constantly ask me if I needed anything. We had this habit of sharing a bit of our day before we fell asleep. One night, after we all wished each other good night and were under the covers, I felt a tug on my shoulder. It was Jonahs.

"You okay?" His face was only somewhat visible in the darkness.

"I'm good. Just wanted to say something else before you fell asleep."

"What?" I asked, my curiosity piqued.

"No matter what people say about your scar, you'll always

be a damn hero to me," he whispered.

Sawyer rushed a little faster.

"Thank you," I said.

"People can be mean," he declared.

"Life can be mean. I've gotten used to Mom making me breakfast and lunch at home, but pretty soon I'm going to have to be content with cafeteria food again." I sighed. "See how cruel life can be?" I joked.

"Just don't forget what I said, okay?"

"I won't."

He released a ragged breath. "All of this will make sense someday. I know it will."

Own Your Story

SEPTEMBER 1986

It was my first day back at Evergreen Middle School. The entire house got up early since Dad expected us to be gathered around the breakfast table by six thirty for a ten-minute Bible study and review of the day's upcoming events. Everyone disliked being up before the sun. On the days we struggled to wake up, he'd blast "Oh, What A Beautiful Mornin'" from the musical *Oklahoma!* at full volume. You'd think he'd extend a little mercy toward me after the surgery, but no, I had to be at the table along with everyone else. The faster we gathered, the sooner that song shut off.

I wore the best things I had in my wardrobe: a jean jacket, dark blue sweater, jeans, and my Vans. I brushed my teeth, grabbed my puffer gray jacket, and cautiously made my way upstairs. I couldn't walk much, and if I moved a lot, my lungs would remind me to take it slow by their inability to take in enough oxygen. To no one's surprise, I was the last one to sit at the table.

Dad asked Dan to pray before we all headed out. Halfway

through, his words turned into determined snores. All the siblings looked at each other, suppressing our laughs. Once Dad noticed the culprit for the sudden silence, he jumped to the rescue. "And may we all do what's right, remember who we are, and return home with honor," he finished with a straight face. "Amen," he said loudly and banged a fist on the table, the act startling my brother out of his sleep.

"We were really deep in prayer there, huh?" he asked.

"So deep, Dad," he replied, eyes heavy.

We all shared a laugh.

The blueish tint of my fingertips held my attention as I dunked my spoon into my bowl of Cocoa Puffs. A few parts of my body had adopted the new color palette since the surgery. My lips matched my fingertips, making me look like a walking corpse.

I wondered how much I'd have to walk between classes, worried I might actually faint on my first day. I didn't want to be known as the guy who passed out all the time.

The Unrelated Twins left as soon as they finished eating since their bus arrived early. My other siblings went to the basement to finish getting ready. Once I was done with breakfast, I grabbed a glass of orange juice and sat looking out the window at Mount Olympus. The sun peeked out from behind the summit, covering its surface with shades of red and orange.

"Excited for your first day back?" Mom asked, cleaning up the table.

"I should be the one asking if you're excited to finally be relieved of your teacher duties."

"Don't try to turn this on me." Mom piled the dirty plates and glasses by the sink.

"You know, I'd be more excited if you'd let me take the bus. All my teachers have already been warned about my condition. Can I at least go to school with the other kids?"

"In a few weeks," she said. "It's too soon."

"I keep thinking about what people will say when they discover my new identity." I took a sip of orange juice.

"And what identity is that?"

"I used to be just Paul, the guy with half a heart. Now I'm the dude who survived open-heart surgery and, as a gift, received blue fingertips and a huge scar right down his chest."

Mom leaned against the counter. She stared at me for a while and then said, "Think about the story you get to share. You're not just someone with half a heart. You're someone who's surviving with one—no matter how broken." She laced her fingers. "I'm pretty sure no one else at that school will be able to say the same. And if they can't see beauty in that, then you keep on living your life until they do."

I chugged down the rest of the orange juice, trying to undo the knot that had formed in my throat.

"Our instincts tell us to run away from what others think

makes us weak," she continued. "I say embrace it and use it as your strength. The prouder you are of your story, the weaker the eyes of the critic."

I chuckled and folded my arms. "You're the wife of a journalist."

"And proud of it." A wide smile appeared on her face. "And even prouder to have raised all of you."

We headed out as soon as she finished cleaning the table. The crisp fall air greeted my cheeks as we walked to our white Dodge Station Wagon. I always had my nose prepared before getting in. My older siblings would occasionally forget a half-eaten sandwich, or some other stinky food, under the seats. One time, we found one so old it was completely covered in mold. To my relief, the car smelled fine. The radio came on as soon as Mom backed out of the driveaway, playing some cheesy slow dance song. The keyboard sounded like an alarm clock and the drums played the same thing over and over again.

"Wow, I'm still recovering from heart surgery here." I ejected the tape and searched her small collection of Elton John and John Denver for the emergency tape I kept in the car. It wasn't long until I spotted the white cover with a sketch of a life preserver.

"Paul, that was good music!"

"I'm sorry. Mind if I play DJ while you drive?" I put in my tape, my ears relieved when a verse of Rush's "The Fountain of Lamneth" started playing.

"Do we have to listen to that this early in the morning?" she asked with an eyeroll.

"Come on, Mom, listen to the words."

> *Look…the mist is rising*
> *And the sun is peaking through*
> *See, the steps grow lighter*
> *As I reach their final few*
> *Hear, the dancing waters*
> *I must be drawing near*
> *Feel, my heart is pounding*
> *With embattled hope and fear*

I sang along, observing the streaks of pink and purple that colored the sky.

School was a fifteen-minute drive from our house. Sawyer picked up speed at the sight of the other kids in front of the building. Seeing all the cute girls in skirts, showing just enough of their summer tan, was a sight for sore eyes—especially for someone who spent the last month quarantined in a house staring at his parents and siblings.

"Have a good first day." Mom ejected my cassette.

"Thanks," I said, getting out of the car. "Enjoy your music."

I tucked my hands in the front pockets of my jacket and

walked past the other kids, head down.

I was expected at the main office. Mrs. Alberline greeted me before I even had a chance to say hello. She looked at me doe-eyed when handing me my class schedule. She repeatedly tilted her head to the side, talking like I was a lost kitten. I also tilted my head, not because I felt sorry for her, but because I kept thinking about how much makeup she needed to get her eyelids the exact shade of blue as my lips.

My first three periods were close to my homeroom, which spared me from walking. I was happy to see a few familiar faces in the hall, but it was just my luck that none of my previous classmates were in my first classes.

My dad's profession gave our family some local fame. Everyone in the area had seen him on TV and knew the Cardall family. The problem was I didn't know the majority of them. I wondered if the kids were staring because they knew me, knew my dad, or because they wanted to know why I looked dead.

Concentrating on the teachers was a hard task when my mind was busy being self-conscious. A few kids chattered while others passed notes when the teacher wasn't looking. Did they talk about me? Did they know me?

I walked out into the hall after third period, looking for room 305. Sawyer skipped a beat, sending a chill down my body, when I realized I had to walk to the other end of the school.

I grabbed the straps of my backpack, suddenly aware of

how heavy my books were. But I was determined to make it without fainting, determined not to be distracted by how easy it was for other kids, and determined not to suffer thinking about it anymore. I walked down the hall with even breaths, proud of my progress. But my sudden rush of courage was drowned out by a sign on the wall with the numbers 300-325 and an arrow pointing up a flight of stairs.

I stood at the foot of the stairs, breathing already a struggle. I glanced at the hall crowded with students and back at what seemed to be a mountain before me. I held on to the rail and took the first couple of steps. The other kids rushed past me, talking and chattering.

My back pressed against the wall halfway through the first flight, my lungs clawing for breath. I slammed my eyes shut and whispered, "You got this."

I carried on and took in a long breath after I hit the last step on the half-way landing. On the wall was another sign with those same numbers and an arrow pointing up—a reminder my struggle wasn't over.

Everything started spinning. My grasp tightened around the rail, knuckles white. I tried to even out my breaths in an attempt to not faint. At least someone was bound to help me if I passed out and rolled down the steps. The other kids kept on rushing past me; I guess I was doing a good job hiding my struggle since none offered to help.

I decided to look at the situation like my mile swim. Even if others were going much faster than me, I could still make it to the end. The late bell rang. I just wouldn't be on time.

It didn't matter that I was late; I was determined to beat the giant. Step by step, breath by breath, I reached the end. Relief filled me when I spotted the door right by the stairs with my new favorite number: 305.

My lungs took in another breath. I walked inside the classroom, clearly interrupting the teacher's introduction to the lesson. I headed to the back, hoping to find a seat, but the only one available was near the front.

All eyes were on me.

"Are you alright?" asked the teacher as soon as I sat down.

"Um, hey," I replied, palms sweaty.

"Paul, right?" She narrowed her dark brown eyes, standing in front of me. She wore a plaid dress that went down to her knees, its pattern in red, green, and blue. Her dark curls fell over her shoulder, guiding my eyes to a brooch on her chest shaped like a butterfly.

"Yeah."

"Are you okay?"

A knot formed in my throat. I tried to contain it, but it came undone.

Great, just great, I thought.

Her face blurred behind a few stubborn tears forming in my eyes. I took in a sharp breath, hoping the action could stop them from breaking free. Everyone's eyes were on me, piercing my skin. After this episode, I was going to sit alone during lunch for the rest of the year for sure.

"Come with me," she said, before turning to the class. "I'll be back in a few minutes. Please act like adults, or I'll see you all in detention."

Mumbles erupted.

Every single kid watched as she led me out of the room.

"I can't go far," I said once we stepped into the hall.

"We're not going too far." She pointed to a door a few feet ahead, next to the library. "We're going in there."

"What's your name?" I wiped my eyes with a wrist.

"Mrs. Dominguez," she replied, leading me into the room. "Welcome to the teacher's lounge. Most kids will never get to see it, but you're special, from what I've heard."

A purple carpet stretched across the floor. There was a vending machine in the corner, a soda machine next to it, and a table with eight chairs at the center. Against one of the walls was a couch covered in white and blue stripes, in front of it a wooden coffee table.

I took a seat as she went to the vending machines. She came back with a bag of potato chips and a can of soda.

"You looked like you needed a pick-me-up." She sat in front of me, opening the can and handing me the bag of chips. For a second, I dwelled on the contradiction of a health teacher giving junk food to her sick student, but I kept my mouth shut and chose to look at it as my reward for surviving those murderous steps.

"Thank you."

"I may be new here, but I know your story," she said.

"I'm glad you know it. It'll save us a conversation." I munched on the chips.

"You're definitely in the spotlight right now."

"Nothing I can do about it," I said with a frown.

"Of course there is. Be proud of whatever it is you're struggling with. Give everyone a chance to see beyond appearance and curiosity. You might be surprised at how much you inspire them."

I took a sip. "The way I see it, those that do know about me are scared to ask questions. Those who don't, stare like I'm an animal on the brink of extinction. I don't ever get a chance to explain."

"But I do." I frowned at her in confusion. "Take control of your story. Tell it in your own words. The world will never be able to rip it away after you do."

"I'll be sure to remember that," I said, wondering how much easier it was to say such things than to act upon them.

"We have to go back to class. I'm afraid I have to rush you a bit."

"No problem," I said with a mouthful of chips, quickly finishing up.

"By the way." She stood up when I was done eating. "Don't

tell them I gave you snacks. They won't get this treatment from me."

"Okay," I said.

We returned to class. Everyone stared like I was Dumbo at the circus. I walked back to my seat, hands in my pockets.

"Before we continue," she started as I was about to sit. "I want to invite Paul up here."

My stomach dropped. I scanned the room, confusion evident in everyone's eyes.

"He has something he'd like to share with all of you," she said, beckoning me to her side with a wave.

I joined her, holding on to my silence as if it could spare me from this moment. But it couldn't. Their faces burned with curiosity.

I told them everything. Though my voice trembled and failed every once in a while, I managed to share my story—to give them the Paul version. From being born with half a heart to my surgery in the summer. Every single one of their faces was taken by surprise as my words carried around the room.

Mrs. Dominguez kept her hand on my shoulder the whole time. Without that, I would have been alone, unconnected, just by myself up there, but that light hand on my shoulder turned me into the bionic hero Jonahs said I was.

Class resumed. Some of the students glanced over their shoulders to stare at the boy with half a heart. A few of the girls waved and smiled. Several of them followed me out after the bell rang.

To my relief, fourth period was on the same floor.

As I walked down the hall, one of them joined me—a beautiful girl with blonde hair and eyes a bright blue. Freckles covered her cheeks, nose, and part of her lips. Her denim jacket had pink hearts embroidered on the right shoulder.

"Hey, Paul." Her smile was contagious, her voice soft and sweet.

"Um…hey." I dragged the *hey* out way more than I needed to. "Hey there."

A few of the students in the hall stared at us.

She laughed and said, "My name's Michelle. Need help with your backpack?"

"I'm alright," I mumbled, struggling to be coherent. "Ask me again if we come across some stairs."

She laughed. "You're funny. Listen, my friends and I have a question for you."

"Your friends?"

She pointed at three girls standing a few feet away. They were all adorable and I seemed to be their main interest.

"Yeah?" I prompted.

"Mind if we call you Purple Plum? A sweet nickname for someone special."

"Ooohhh," erupted in unison from a couple of the kids behind me.

"I mean..." I cleared my throat, blinking repeatedly. "You can call me whatever your healthy heart desires."

She laughed, cheeks flushed.

A few of the students entered the classroom with me, Michelle being one of them. Luckily, she sat in the chair beside mine.

If Sawyer had a face, he'd definitely be sporting a smug smile.

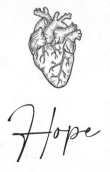

Hope

FEBRUARY 2006

I decided to take a shot at cooking dinner to celebrate Olivia's first day back at work. The menu: roasted chicken, mashed potatoes, gravy, and green beans. I wasn't much of a chef, but I could find my way around the kitchen.

The past few months had been joy and chaos. Olivia never brought up our disagreement over the Christmas concerts again. She picked me up from the airport like nothing had happened. Maybe she was just relieved to have me back so I could help out with Neil. Jonahs also dropped the news that he and Hannah were planning to have a baby. They had delayed their move to Arizona until the end of next year but seemed to be happier than ever. He was also stable, from what he told me.

In our house, diapers piled like pungent mountains, which resulted in about four daily trips to the trash in the freezing weather.

Olivia came down dressed in her blue scrubs.

"I hope you're hungry," I said as she took a seat.

"This is *your* favorite dish." She smirked. "You cooked it for you."

"You'll be surprised at how good this is."

I fixed us both a plate and set them on the table.

"It does look good," she said, fork and knife in hand.

I sat across from her, noticing her vacant stare and her apparent lack of interest in conversation as we ate.

"Are you alright?" I asked.

"I'm okay." She shook her head. "It's just leaving Neil for the first time."

I grabbed her hand. "It'll be fine. You need to do something for you as well."

"I guess." She continued eating. I'm not sure if she tried to conceal the worried expression on her face. If so, she didn't do a good job.

"I could always stop doing music." Guilt clutched Sawyer under my chest. "I know your job is important because we need health insurance, but I could drop everything and find that nine-to-five job. I know you've—"

"No," she admonished. "It's fine. Every parent has to deal with leaving their child at some point." Her brows arched upward. "Some sooner than others, but hey, that's life, and this is what we wanted. We wanted kids. You wanted to make music. I wanted to be with you. It's all part of the package."

"I guess," I mumbled.

"Going to keep working on the new album this evening?" she asked.

"Yes. Going to try to write something. Wish me luck." I smiled.

"Heard from Dr. Kupo yet?"

"Not yet," I said, my smile fading. "I might give him a ring later."

"It's been, what, three weeks since your check-up?" she asked. "Shouldn't they have called by now?"

"I'm sure we would've heard something if my heart was ready to give out. No news is good news."

She was always tense the days after a check-up. I remained grounded—or at least pretended to be so as not to add to her burden. I'd always tell myself that everything was going to be alright. That was a lie I enjoyed believing so I could feel alive.

She picked up her empty plate and placed it by the sink. I followed her into the living room and watched her grab her coat and purse from the coat hanger in the corner.

"Hey." She turned at the sound of my voice. "Neil's proud of you."

"Thank you." She smiled.

Neil's high-pitched screams bellowed as soon as Olivia left. He fussed in his crib, dressed in a blue romper with a dinosaur stamped on his chest.

I took him downstairs, fed him, and put him in the rocker by the piano in the living room. I was working out a few arrangements for a new song when the explosive new ringtone of my flip phone startled me. Neil shuffled in his rocker as I rushed to the kitchen to answer.

"Hello?"

"Hello, this is Dr. Kupo. Is this Paul?"

"Hey, Doc." My gaze flitted around the room.

"How are things? How's Neil?" I sensed a concealed apprehension in his voice.

"Everything is great, but I'm assuming there's more to this call than life updates?"

A nervous chuckle. "I have a few concerns regarding your tests."

Sawyer skipped a beat. "Oh, I thought everything was okay since I didn't hear back for a while."

"It's too early to tell, but I wanted to schedule a few blood tests."

"How soon?" I asked.

"Can you come tomorrow at one?"

"Yes," I mumbled. "I'll be there."

I returned to the piano, my fingers meeting the keys and playing a lower G over and over. That's how I felt with all these tests and follow-ups, like I was a nail and life was the hammer hitting me on the head. The melody eventually progressed into a lullaby in a higher octave. Neil slept beside me as the notes found each other. After about an hour, the song had structure. It told a story. I wanted to live. I wanted to be around for the people I loved. I wanted to hope for a better future.

"Hope," I whispered. "Hope. That's what I'm naming you."

I also needed someone who could help me keep on hoping.

"Hello?"

"Jonahs," I said.

"Paul." There was an edge to his voice. "Are you alright?"

"Yeah, I'm okay. Listen, can you meet me at the clinic tomorrow at one? Dr. Kupo called, and they want to do a few last-minute blood tests. I don't want to tell Olivia. Not yet, anyway."

Silence.

"I'd just like to have someone there with me," I added.

I jumped up from the couch and grabbed my coat as soon as Olivia walked through the door. Neil was in his rocker, playing with his Apatosaurus teething toy.

"Good shift?" I asked, car keys in hand.

"Another pregnant mom on meth lost her baby." She frowned. "Heading out already?"

"I have some errands to run. I'll be back soon. Promise. Call me if you want to talk about it."

Johnny Cash was the soundtrack of the drive.

"It's going to be alright," I repeated out loud. "It's going to be alright."

Jonahs waited in the lobby, dressed in a puffy black jacket, gray beanie, tattered blue jeans, and boots. A real heartthrob. He hugged me the moment I was inside.

"Thank you for coming," I said.

"Of course." He smiled. "Happy to babysit you whenever you need."

The receptionist led me to see Dr. Kupo. Jonahs couldn't go in with me, but just having him around helped me believe things were going to be alright.

Dr. Kupo's hair was perfectly combed to the side. He had a scruff of a beard on his dark face and a scar under his nose from being born with a cleft lip. He attempted to make small talk. I tried hard to read his eyes, hoping the situation wasn't as dire as my mind painted it to be. He sent in a phlebotomist who prepped my arm for more lab work. I still dreaded needles even though I'd seen a million of them. I honestly thought this particular phlebotomist was going to bleed me dry. Six full vials. Maybe she was Dracula.

"I'll call you once I have news," Dr. Kupo said in a flat voice, dismissing me with a handshake.

"How bad?" I said, his hand still in my grasp.

"You know how these things go." He shrugged. "I can't say much until I'm sure."

I had to wait two days for the call to come. Dr. Kupo was blunt. Sawyer had grown into the size of an NFL football and decided to crush my lungs. My medication dosage was going to be increased to extend Sawyer's lifespan. Dr. Kupo said I still had some time and didn't need to be listed as a transplant candidate yet. But that was it. Sawyer had started to fail.

Good News

APRIL 2007

I rushed out to St. Thomas Women's Center when Olivia got home from work to watch Neil—since Neil had started walking, he needed our attention more than ever. I stopped by the store and bought some flowers and a pink helium balloon shaped like a pacifier with the word *Congratulations* across the front. Jonahs and Hannah were about to become parents.

It had been over a year since Dr. Kupo told me Sawyer was beginning to fail. I was still around. Still kicking.

I entered the hospital and asked to see Mrs. Hannah Cardall, going through all the formalities before being led to her room.

Jonahs threw his arms around me as soon as I put the flowers on the table. The bags under his eyes and the wide smile on his face fully showed a man entering fatherhood. Hannah smiled from her bed, their new baby girl in her arms, wrapped in a white blanket, head covered in a pink beanie.

"Hey, Pollyanna," she said as I tied the pink balloon to the foot of the bed. "You have a brand-new niece to spoil. Plenty of gifts are expected."

"And this balloon is her first," I said.

She smirked. "Not a great start."

"Is that what you're naming her?" I smiled. "Pollyanna as a tribute to her amazing uncle Paul?"

Jonahs guffawed.

"Her name is Zoe," Hannah said. "Zoe Cardall."

She looked like Jonahs, her lips and eyes the same shape as his. "I do love the both of you, but I came here to revel in the masterpiece you've created."

"You want to hold her?" Hannah asked.

Jonahs pressed his lips together. "You think he has the experience?"

"I'm ready to school you on how to be a dad." I bent down and gently picked her up. She remained still, sleeping. "Hey, Zoe. I love you very much, but you're the reason most of the family will no longer remember my birthday since you were born a day before it."

"Consider yourself lucky." Jonahs put a hand on my shoulder. "I'd give anything for people to forget mine."

We chatted for a half hour or so before nurses came in and took Zoe back to the nursery and Hannah was on the verge of sleep. Hugs went all around as I headed out. I was happy and proud of my brother, but with Jonahs, there was always something. His eyes reflected whatever struggle was going on inside. Was there more to the reason why they had postponed their move?

Jonahs was eager to escape the Cardall compound when he hit his teenage years. He'd randomly disappear with his friends, only to come home days later from some grand adventure. My parents would have a fit every time it happened. Maybe he was trying to fill a void or struggling to run from one.

Ever since the episode in 2005, I'd catch myself thinking about the many things I could say to him.

Neil rushed my way when I walked inside the house. His big smile pushed all my thoughts away. He had on a blue T-Rex shirt and a yellow sticky note stuck to his front. Olivia leaned against the wall, arms crossed, and a smile on display.

"Hey, buddy!" I picked him up and gave him a hug. "What's this?" I plucked the note from his chest, reading it aloud, "I'm going to be a big brother." The world stopped as I processed what I had read. "Wait, what? You're…"

"We're having a baby!" Olivia said, crying as she made her way over to me.

Sawyer wanted to break free from his bony cage. "We're having…we're—"

I set Neil back down. He darted around the house, yelling, "Brotha! Brotha! I be big brotha!"

"Our family is growing." Olivia laid her head on my shoulder. "The doctor said I'm thirteen weeks in."

"You've seen one already?"

"Consider this payback, mister." She smiled.

"This will happen for us," I said.

Nothing to Worry About

JUNE 2007

I woke up before the sun and retreated to my home office to read some emails—most of them from fans sharing intimate stories of how my music helped them. They ranged from people who were inspired to pursue their passions to those who were on the verge of taking their own lives, only to have a song of mine help them believe in the future again.

More than ever before, new listeners were discovering my music. Pandora Radio featured all my albums and suggested them to millions every day. I tried my best to reply to as many as I could.

The last email was confirmation the day was off to a great start. It was a report from the marketing agency overseeing my campaigns. All my projects, including the latest, *Songs of Praise*, were getting incredible radio play, especially the song "Redeemer." There was a graph attached, depicting a noticeable rise in listeners after they executed all their marketing ideas.

Sawyer had managed to remain stable after news of his

failure last year. I put on some weight, the swelling went down, and all tests assured me Sawyer still had plenty of time to live on.

But it was a rare occasion; Olivia was home on a Saturday. Our day was going to consist of television, plenty of carbs, and popcorn.

I went downstairs to work on new music. I had to get a jump start on a new album—especially after the reports I received. The melodies started as a whisper since I didn't want to wake anyone up, but my excitement got the best of me, and the entire house was awake before eight.

We all had German pancakes and Cocoa Puffs for breakfast. Neil turned his meal into a face cream, smearing the syrup around his lips then licking his fingers.

"Babies coming?" Neil asked in a sweet voice.

"Very soon," I told him. "They aren't ready to leave Mommy's belly yet."

"When?" he insisted, picking up a soggy cereal from his bowl and eating it.

"You'll know when it's time, champ," Olivia replied.

We gathered in the living room with a bowl of popcorn, ready to spend the day watching Scooby-Doo. We had even picked out special pajamas for the occasion. Neil's were white with lion cubs scattered over it. Olivia's purple and covered in flowers. Mine were blue, stamped with horses. Neil then proceeded to use most of the couch cushions to build himself a tower.

"Neil, are you planning on staying in your tower the whole day?" Olivia asked, fixing her hair behind her ears.

"Yes," Neil replied from his cushioned fortress. "This my house, Mommy."

Olivia and I chuckled. She looked radiant, her small bump in view. I always thought she looked even more beautiful when pregnant. An irony considering our past experiences.

None of us had even dared to brush our hair. This was our official lazy day. Neil's efforts to keep his tower stable were way more entertaining than whatever was on TV.

The day went on. The only time we left the couch was to fix a few ham and cheese sandwiches for lunch. Neil, however, stayed in his tower, wrapped in a blue blanket, surrounded by dinosaurs and cars.

"We should watch something different," I mentioned. "My head hurts from watching this dog."

"Couldn't agree more." Olivia smiled, but a sudden look of concern invaded her face. She tossed the bowl of popcorn on my lap. Her complexion paled as her eyes bulged like basketballs. She jumped up from the couch with a gasp.

"Everything okay?" I asked, Sawyer thumping.

"Yes, just need to use the bathroom. Be back soon." There was an edge to her voice as she rushed upstairs.

For the next couple of minutes, Neil kept climbing on the edge of the couch and jumping on the pillow tower, giggling and begging me to watch his every move.

The sound of rushed footsteps coming from the stairs stole my breath. I jumped up, alarmed, the popcorn spilling on the floor.

"Olivia?"

"Paul." She paraded into the living room with tears. "I'm bleeding."

We were still in our pajamas when we rushed out of the house and jumped in the car. I called Mom and explained the situation. She didn't say much, but judging by her uneven breaths, thousands of words and thoughts came to mind. I asked her to meet us at the hospital so she could take Neil for the day. Every second felt rushed, yet lasted an eternity. My eyes swerved between the road, Olivia, and Neil, who was in his car seat with a Triceratops in hand.

My grip tightened around the steering wheel. *Not again. Not now.* Olivia's face was pale, lips colorless. A blue towel was wrapped around her waist to conceal the blood stain. Her hands were pressed over her stomach as tears escaped her eyes.

"Mommy, don't cry," Neil said.

"Oh, sweetie," Olivia said in a broken voice. "Mommy has to cry now, but she'll be okay soon."

I turned into the hospital parking lot. Mom stood by the double doors. She waved once she spotted us. I left the car by the curb with the flashers on.

"Unlock the back," my mother yelled, her hand already on the door handle.

"Grandma!" Neil said, releasing the dinosaur in his grasp and extending his arms toward her. She unbuckled Neil from the car seat and held him. Neil's immediate reaction was to lay his head on my mom's shoulder.

"Call me the moment you hear anything," she demanded.

"Promise."

Olivia and I rushed to the front desk. The receptionist on the other side stood to her feet. She had freckles across her cheeks, eyes as green as the first leaves of spring. A brooch shaped like the face of a cat was pinned to her white coat along with a name tag that read Rebecca.

I explained Olivia's symptoms, hopeful we were going to be seen at once. But we were asked to take a seat. I insisted we see a doctor right away, but her request was the same.

I watched the clock on the wall, every second an age. The door beside the front desk burst open. A woman approached, thick-framed glasses on her face.

"Olivia Cardall," she called out.

I grabbed Olivia's hand and helped her stand. The towel around her waist drooped, but she managed to catch it before it revealed the scarlet nightmare.

The woman attempted to keep a cheery face, but her efforts failed.

"I'm Nurse Ana," she said. "Please come with me."

We followed her into a room with white walls. To my right was a bed and beside it an ultrasound machine.

"Take a seat on the bed," she demanded as she sat on the rolling chair. "Unbutton your shirt and lie down."

Olivia handed me the blood-soaked towel and her shirt.

Ana smeared Olivia's belly with gel and ran the transducer over her stomach. I struggled to breathe. Every single one of the nurse's movements sent Sawyer on a spree.

I observed Ana's facial expressions as if watching a horror movie. Was she going to frown? Maybe she'd sigh in relief after realizing my twins were alive.

Ana's gaze shifted from Olivia back to the screen while sliding the transducer. She repeated the action a few times, until placing the magic wand back in its hook.

She rolled her seat a few inches away from Olivia and smiled.

"Your babies are fine," she declared. "The boy and the girl are alive and well."

Olivia and I glanced at each other, laughter bursting out of the both of us.

"What about their hearts?" I asked. "Everything okay there?"

"Both are beating just fine."

I squeezed Olivia's hand. She returned the gesture.

Ana's words steadied Sawyer. Olivia's smile remained intact.

We were told to head home and take it easy until an update on the cause of the bleeding.

The phone rang at exactly ten a.m. the next day while I was at the piano working on the new album. The results confirmed a large blood clot in the uterus. Olivia was to stay in absolute bedrest until her follow-up appointment the next week.

I picked up Neil and headed upstairs to share the results with Olivia.

"This is terrifying," she whispered, sitting up in bed. "I see things like this at the hospital all the time. I'm just waiting for another miscarriage to happen—"

"It won't," I said, sitting beside her, Neil in my arms. "I promise it won't."

Neil crawled out of my lap, reclining his head against Olivia. "Even you can't promise me that, Paul," she said, her arm around Neil. "This isn't how I pictured my life." Emptiness engulfed her eyes. "Why is it so hard?"

"We have good news, Olivia." I held her hand between my own. "You just need to rest. The twins are fine."

"Mind calling my dad for me? I don't want to deal with telling him."

"Of course," I whispered.

I dialed the number with trembling fingers.

Her father was usually a gentle man, patient and kind. He was always joyful when spending time with Neil and Olivia, but I knew he looked at me as the reason his daughter suffered so much. He wasn't wrong.

"Hello, sweetheart," he answered after a few rings, his voice unwavering. "How are you?"

"Mr. Allen, it's actually Paul," I said, chest tight.

"Well, hey Paul." His voice took on a tone of concern. "Is everything okay?"

I broke the news, feeling like Sawyer was being pressed down by a bulldozer the whole time. There I was again telling him of Olivia's suffering.

He was mostly quiet during the call, reacting to most of my words with long sighs.

"Need me to drive out to be with her?" he asked in a monotone voice.

"No, we should be okay. I'll let you know once we have more news."

"Paul, just..." A brief pause. "Just don't die on my daughter."

He hung up before I had the chance to respond.

I gazed at the phone, prepared to call him back, but then I thought of Neil. How would I feel if he were to choose a partner in my frail condition? Maybe I'd share the same thoughts he did. Those same concerns would be the ghosts I'd see every night.

"Don't die on my daughter," I repeated.

It was an unusual week. Mom and my older sister, Kirsten, came over to help take care of Neil. They took turns babysitting while I ran errands, attended business meetings, and tried to work on new music for my next album. Olivia stayed in bed most of the time, eager to return to her routine by week's end.

To our family's relief, the follow up appointment brought positive results. The blood clot had dissolved; Olivia could resume her normal routine.

But just when we thought we had reached the end of this journey, Olivia passed a huge blood clot a week later.

The ultrasound confirmed our worst nightmare. The heart rate of our girl remained strong, but our boy's was slowing down. The doctor told us there wasn't much to do but wait. We were scheduled to return for another ultrasound in two days. Before we left the hospital, he made it clear that both babies might be dead the next time we came back.

The drive to the ultrasound appointment was a quiet one. Olivia stroked her belly while humming the melody of "Our Love." Her hazel eyes were set on the luscious summer landscape. There wasn't a single cloud in the sky. Mount Olympus dominated in the distance.

"It's going to be fine," I said. "We have to stay positive."

"You keep saying that." She sighed, pushing her hair behind her ears. "I want to believe it, but no, Paul, it'll *never* be alright."

"I'm telling you it will," I insisted.

"Every time we take a step forward, we go back four. It's one thing after another. Our lives are apparently all sorrow and only a few moments of bliss." She sniffed. "I'm tired."

"That's nothing compared to what we have with Neil. What are you saying?"

"This will be his life. One tragedy after another. That terrifies me." She pressed the heels of her hands over her eyes and whispered to herself, "God, I can't— All…all this…uncertainty. Why do you take me down this path?"

She had been reckless in choosing me: a musician with a bad heart. I was not a sound investment for a girl who'd already been through enough as a child. I was uncertainty. There seemed to be some unseen force out there that had decided to crush my marriage with hopeless dreams of a normal life.

Entering the hospital felt like entering a death chamber. I hated the smell: iodine, alcohol, flesh, death. I knew I probably wasn't leaving this place with good news. To our surprise, the nurse who had seen us a few weeks ago greeted us and led us to the room.

"You may take a seat, Mr. Cardall," said Ana, waving to a chair pressed against the wall as Olivia lay on the bed.

"No, I think I'll stand for this."

"Suit yourself," she said, a grim expression on her face.

I braced for the worst when she placed the transducer on Olivia's stomach. Ana frowned, sliding it around repeatedly. The corner of her lips trembled into a smile as her attention shifted between the screen and Olivia's belly.

"Is everything okay?" I asked, afraid of her answer.

"Yes, actually. Yes." Ana's smile was contagious. "They're fine. They're both fine."

"No!" Olivia's head jolted up from the bed.

"Both heart rates are stable. Everything's great."

"Thank God." I pressed a nail into my thumb just to ensure I wasn't dreaming. The pain convinced me it was real.

"So they're fine?" Olivia asked.

"You have nothing to worry about," Ana affirmed.

Our Children

JULY 2007

"Paul. Paul!"

Olivia's blaring voice woke me up and jolted me to my feet. I glanced at my flip phone, still a bit disoriented. It was midnight. I had fallen asleep on the floor of Neil's room, next to his new toddler bed shaped like a race car. I'd gotten used to this new routine since he started having night terrors.

"Paul, come here!" Olivia shouted.

I ran into our room, my pulse pounding in my ears. The world stopped after I turned on the light switch. My eyes bulged at the image of our sheets turned scarlet.

"It's bad. And the cramps"—she winced, sweat beading down her brow—"are really strong tonight."

"I'll call my mom and have her pick up Neil at the hospital."

We rushed out of the house without a fresh change of clothes. Olivia's white blood-soaked pajamas stared back at me. Neil was somewhat awake as we transitioned him to the car, his hair was spiked up like a mohawk.

Neil fell back to sleep once we were on our way. Olivia trembled, her teeth pressing down into her lip as she groaned. It was like riding the most frightening roller coaster—one with broken tracks and wild turns. I wondered what waited for us at the end of it: a drop, a climb, or a dark stillness.

Mom was parked right in front of the ER, Dad sitting beside her.

I quickly handed over Neil and helped Olivia into the ER, rushing to the receptionist behind the front desk.

"My wife, she's pregnant and bleeding. We need help!"

"Please stay calm, sir," she said while typing something on her computer. "You're in the best place you could be in a situation like this." The waiting room was packed with patients.

"We're very busy tonight as you can see." Her attention remained on her computer. "The on-call doctor will see you soon. Please take a seat."

"Take a seat?" My cheeks flushed. Olivia leaned forward, using the edge of the desk to hold herself up. Her face scrunched as she moaned. "Look at her. We have to see a doctor right away. We can't wait!"

"You need to wait, sir." She stiffened her posture. "He's currently with a patient. I'm sorry, but there's a process. The doctor will be with you as soon as possible."

"This is ridiculous," I contested. Sawyer wanted to jump out of my chest and strangle the insensitive woman.

The bleeding continued as we waited. The chair was stained red, blood trickling down its wooden legs, spreading on the floor. Olivia trembled and shuddered. Her grip around my hand was so tight I thought she was going to break it. My eyes flitted around the room, stunned there was no one available to help. All watched in horror and shock.

I marched to the front desk after waiting for almost half an hour.

"We need to see a doctor right away, for crying out loud!" My hand slammed on the desk. "We've had miscarriages before. This cannot wait."

"We're doing the best we can." The receptionist's voice wavered. "We have people here who've been waiting longer—

"Are you serious?" Blood rushed to my face.

A woman stood up from her chair, an eye patch on her face. "His wife is bleeding!" she shouted in a hoarse voice. "She can have my turn. She needs a doctor."

A nurse emerged from the door behind the receptionist.

"What's going on—" Her jaw dropped at the sight of me. "Paul?"

"Yes?" I said, confused.

"Purple Plum?" She frowned.

"Do we know each other?" I asked.

"It's me, Michelle from middle school, remember?"

I squinted at the memory of my first day back in school after my endocarditis surgery. I recalled the sound of her voice, the blue of her eyes, and the freckles on her face. She was the girl who nicknamed me Purple Plum. She had transferred schools a few days later, and I never heard from her again.

"Michelle! Please, please help us." I rushed back to Olivia and grabbed her hand. "My wife's bleeding. We've been waiting for—"

"Get me a wheelchair now!" The receptionist stood at the sound of Michelle's blaring words. "Now, please!"

"I was just following proto—"

"Now!"

The receptionist appeared seconds later with a wheelchair.

Michelle rolled it toward us and wheeled us into a room with three other patients and a vacant bed. Olivia was pale, tear streaks stained her cheeks. The blood on her white pants resembled a crime scene.

"I'll get the doctor right away," Michelle said as a team of nurses stormed inside the room and closed the curtains around us, helping Olivia undress.

A doctor joined them seconds later.

"Dr. McConkie, we need you now!" yelled one of the nurses. He stood in the way, blocking my view.

They laid her on the bed after she was clothed in her blue hospital gown.

My head moved left and right in an attempt to see what was going on. "Move, move!" I shouted at the nurse in front of me. "I can't see anything!"

Olivia let out a scream.

The room fell quiet as I shoved the nurse to the side. Sawyer stopped. The world stopped. On the bed was an almost fully developed baby girl, encircled by a blood stain. She was so small she could fit in my hand. Her fingers and toes were fully formed, heart-shaped lips ready to cry, but still.

"No, no, no, no." I pressed my hands to my head, turning to McConkie, and then scanning the mask-covered faces of every single nurse in the room. "Can't you do something?" I begged. "Please?"

"She's gone, Paul," Dr. McConkie said. "I'll have an ultrasound machine brought in so we can check on the other."

A nurse wrapped our daughter in cloth and put her on a table by the foot of the bed. Everyone left the room. Mumbles and chatter echoed from the other three patients on their beds.

My daughter's lifeless body was soaked in blood. My mind gazed into a future that could have been. What would her cry have sounded like? Would she have loved music like her daddy?

Olivia whimpered quietly. Her blood-smeared clothes were a bundle on the floor.

I remained rooted to the spot, still as a rock in the desert. Dr. McConkie wheeled in the ultrasound machine.

"Hurry up," I said, defeated.

He examined Olivia's belly, and as he was about to run the transducer over her stomach, she released another gut-wrenching scream. Another blood clot. The body of another baby followed.

I closed my eyes and counted to five in my head, hoping I'd wake up after I was done. But I didn't. My children were still dead in front of me.

Dr. McConkie wrapped him, laying him beside his dead sister. He left the room without uttering a single word.

A frightening silence. Olivia and I alone. We stared into each other's eyes for a while. A dark ocean of agony drowned out the light in her soul. I ached to find words to fill the void, but death was the only answer between us.

I sat on the edge of the bed, observing their corpses.

Michelle came into the room but left as soon as she glanced at our dead twins.

"Sarah and Abel," Olivia said, voice caught in her throat. I turned to her. "Their names."

"Our children," I mumbled. "Sarah and Abel."

I wanted to take in every moment I had with them. I wondered what they'd say if they could speak. Maybe they'd tell us how they were suffering inside her belly for a while. Two nurses stormed into the room, disrupting my thoughts. They took their tiny bodies away.

It had been a week since the traumatic incident. Olivia kept to herself most days, bursting into tears again and again. I tried consoling her, but I knew there was no way out of this void, only through. Neil remained his excited self, playing with dinosaurs, building towers out of pillows, and humming made-up songs. To him, he was lucky to have both parents at home for a whole week.

Our family and friends overwhelmed us with love every single day, constantly calling to check on us. A few wanted to visit, but we asked for privacy.

Dr. McConkie called to apologize for not asking if we wanted to have our twins prepared for burial. He explained the hospital takes care of them if they're less than twenty-five weeks old—something I knew; something Olivia knew. But hearing it from him made the pain even more real.

I sat at the piano, replaying the past few days, my thoughts filtering into songs. Neil was going to be dropped off at my parents' so we could go on another trip to the hospital. Our family probably deserved some kind of award for all the hospital visits. Olivia needed a dilation and curettage—or D&C, a procedure to clear her uterus from any remnants of the pregnancy.

My fingers suddenly abandoned the keys. I looked around the silent room, imagining Abel and Sarah running around and playing with Neil. I wanted a life of peace for my family and me but wanting wasn't enough. The keys were under my fingers once again, my left hand in an arpeggio flow in the lower register. My right hand joined in as I closed my eyes, darkness my companion. As images of an impossible future flooded my mind, I composed a song I eventually called "Monday Morning." The melody reflected the things I wanted. I wanted to hold on to hope, but Sawyer's every thump reminded me of everyone's downfall, my twins and my own.

Olivia appeared dressed in a white robe, wet hair running down her shoulders. She held Neil's hand while approaching the piano.

At the sight of my smile, Neil let go of Olivia and ran to me, the melody exciting his little heart. He tapped my arm, signaling me to scoot over so he could sit on the bench with me.

Olivia retreated upstairs without a single word.

"Daddy," Neil said with pouted lips. My hands left the keys, silence settling.

"Yes, buddy?" I wrapped an arm around his shoulders.

His broad smile revealed his crooked teeth. "Daddy, when babies arrive?"

The question was a blade to my heart, a sharp breath my

weapon against the knot that formed in my throat. The sunlight spilling from the window lightened his brown eyes. I stared deep into them. "God needed them for something really special. So they couldn't stay." It was the best—and probably the worst—explanation I could find at that moment.

"Why?" A frown creased his forehead.

"I don't know," I replied. "All I know is they had to go be with Him for a while. But you'll meet them someday."

He folded his arms with great determination. "They don't want to see me?"

My lungs pulled in a breath. "Oh, Neil, it's not that. Sometimes babies are so comfortable in their momma's bellies, they decide to make that their only home while on this Earth."

"Oh," he cooed.

"And when they're born, they don't open their eyes or cry because they're already with God in Heaven." I fixed the collar of his little polo shirt. "But the good news is that we'll all get to meet them someday."

"Okay." His hands dropped to his lap. "Will they like me?"

"Neil," I whispered. "They already love you."

"Okay!" He ran to the couch and tossed the cushions on the floor.

I watched as he started building his pillow tower. But then he halted, two pillows in his grasp. His gaze turned to me. "Only you, me, and Momma live in the house now."

"That's correct," I replied, wishing life had given Olivia and me what we wanted.

For a quick second, I envied my son's innocence. The only comfort he needed was his father's voice. He believed what I said without a doubt. My explanation was vague and full of plot holes but enough to calm his little mind.

The melody of "Redeemer" filled the house as my fingers danced over the keys. My son's giggles joined the melody.

Olivia walked downstairs and joined Neil in the living room, ready for her appointment. She watched Neil play with the cushions and pillows from her seat on the arm of the couch.

"Mom, it's a house for us." Neil's voice complemented the music.

"It looks beautiful." Olivia smiled.

"Babies will come one day." Neil fixed a pillow at the bottom of his tower. "You'll see."

Olivia's posture stiffened. "They will?" she asked, clearly holding back tears.

"Yes, Mommy." Neil looked at her with determination, his hair a mess. "I want to be ready!"

I expected Olivia to break down. But instead, she knelt in front of Neil and held him by the waist. "We'll meet them, and we'll all be together. And when that happens, we'll all build a house for us to live in. But let's finish building later. We're going to see Grandma and Grandpa now."

Neil rested his head on Olivia's shoulder.

The three of us hopped in the car, Neil strapped in his chair. He hummed and sang his own songs until we got to my parents' house. Silence loomed between Olivia and me after we dropped him off.

"In the mood for some music?" I asked in an attempt to break the tension.

"Sure," she answered in a flat voice, nibbling on the side of her thumb.

I turned on the radio and pressed play on whatever CD was inside.

Olivia shuffled in her seat and let out a long sigh as Rush's "Tears" came on.

What would touch me deeper
Tears that fall from eyes that only cry?
Would it touch you deeper
Than tears that fall from eyes
That know why?
A lifetime of questions
Tears on your cheek
I tasted the answers
And my body was weak
For you
The truth

"Are you alright?" I lowered the volume after the chorus came to an end.

"The thought of going back there..." She pressed her eyes shut.

"One day, we'll be going back to the hospital for the birth of our second child." She stilled at my words. "And when that day comes, that child will be worth all the problems that don't make sense right now."

My affirmation was met with the usual questionnaire as to why our lives were so broken. She questioned our trials, our suffering, and spoke as if the future held nothing but darkness and toil. Eventually she turned up the volume of the music, lips sealed in silence.

I remained in the waiting room while they saw Olivia. They assured us it wasn't going to be a long procedure. The patients around me sparked unwelcome memories of my twins wrapped in cloths covering their frail bodies.

I paced around, visited the water fountain, stared at the paintings, read the brochures scattered on the coffee tables, and even grabbed a few snacks from the vending machine. How long until the memories became scars? How long until Sawyer gave out completely? How long until it was Olivia's turn to wait for me while I was in an operating room?

Into the Fire

AUGUST 1987

"Paul," said a distant voice while something shook me by the shoulder. I searched the darkness with eyes half-opened. "Paul, time to get up. It's five a.m." I recognized my mom's voice. "You have to get ready."

I rubbed my eyes to the sound of her fading footsteps. I eventually got up and wobbled my way to the bathroom without bothering to turn the light on. I had dreaded this day for a year. I was going back to that freaking hospital.

My reflection in the dark mirror stared back at me, but the scar on my chest made everything else fade away.

They had to pry me open again. Sawyer was going to literally see the light of day one more time. Doctors explained the surgery would help my blood flow smoother so it could pick up oxygenated cells. I was conflicted when they said my blueish fingertips and lips would look normal after this. I kind of enjoyed being called Purple Plum.

I showered and crept back into the bedroom to get dressed. Dan and Jonahs were fast asleep in their beds. It was still dark outside. My lungs begged for oxygen every few steps. Dressing and walking upstairs for breakfast took all the wind out of me.

My parents chattered in the kitchen, the table already set with a jar of orange juice, Cocoa Puffs, milk, and waffles. The downside was that I wasn't allowed to have anything.

"Morning, Paul," Dad said. His graying hair was combed to the side, perfectly sprayed into place. There wasn't a single wrinkle on his white button-down shirt. A quick glance and one would assume he was studio-ready, a moment's notice from appearing on television to report the news.

"Morning." I sat in front of Mom as she poured herself some Cocoa Puffs.

"Ready for today?" Dad asked.

"Sure." I shrugged.

My *sure* was like a ticking grenade.

Mom gently laid a hand over my arm and said, "It's just another step for you to get better."

"And another addition to my scar collection." I said, watching her dunk the spoon into her bowl. Every time she munched on the cereal, I heard the ticking of the grenade growing louder and faster. *Tick. Tick. Tick.* Then it finally exploded. "Why do I have to go through all this? The other day, I was thinking how ninety nine point nine percent of my friends will never in their lifetimes experience what I have this past year. I should be worried about starting freshman year soon, not my heart seeing the light of day again."

"I get that you're scared," Dad said in a calming voice. "I would be too. But our God has scars. And right now, you're in His fire. Things can get warm, but you'll never be burned."

I scoffed. "Why do I have to be the only one in this family to walk through this so-called fire? That makes no sense. I could've inherited some heart disease in my fifties because of how much Cocoa Puffs and banana bread I eat." My chest raised with a ragged breath.

"Fire refines gold." Dad seemed too calm as he drank his juice.

I shrugged in response.

"The impurities of gold are removed when it's thrown in the fire," he continued.

"Dad, don't take this the wrong way." I scratched the side of my head. "But you seem too calm. Like, very calm. Your son is about to be cut open so doctors can play house with his heart and get a nice paycheck for it."

He laced his fingers and brought them to his chin. "Let me tell you something that only your mother knows. You can believe it or think it was just a dream. Do whatever you want with what I'm about to share. After your first surgery when you were born, I heard a few doctors whispering in the hall. They said you were not going to make it. They probably didn't know I could hear them. The words killed me." His eyes glistened. "I went outside. I imagined your mom hearing the news. How devastated the family would be. But something unexpected calmed my storm."

"What was that?" I asked.

"I heard your adult voice in the wind."

I frowned at his answer. Dad had never been one to talk fantasy. He was too much of a reporter for it.

"It's true." Dad smiled after noticing my expression. "You whispered, *'Don't worry, Dad. I'll be alright.'* And that stopped my fear."

"Just like that?" I snapped my fingers.

"Just like that." He repeated the gesture. "You assured me you were going to make it."

"It takes as much effort to doubt as it does to believe, Paul," Mom added. "At some point, you have to make your choice."

"Everything will be alright." Dad's smile remained intact. "The fire doesn't last forever."

Walking into the hospital was like entering a prison. I knew I was going to be in there a while. My parents and I were led to a room with a few nurses already waiting inside. I was asked to strip and put on the turquoise gown neatly folded on top of the bed. I pulled the white curtain shut to have some privacy while changing.

But then I stopped. The scar on my chest was reflected in the mirror hanging on the wall. It held my attention for a few seconds, until I decided to look at my face—something I hadn't done as often in the past year. The dark circles around my eyes were bluer and deeper than I remembered. I nibbled on my blueish lips and gazed at my fingertips, ready to say goodbye to the billboards that showed the world Sawyer was sick.

I slid the curtain open. My parents smiled, both sitting on two chairs lined up against the wall. A nurse was next to them, half of her face hidden behind a surgical mask. Her round hazel eyes bore into mine.

"I'm going to need you to lie down." Her sweet voice made me think of cotton candy.

I did as she requested. Goosebumps spread across my body as my back met the cold surface of the surgical bed. She inserted the IV. I winced at the familiar feeling of the sharp metal slowly sliding into my body.

"Ready to do this?" she asked.

"Sure." I said, even though I wanted to urge everyone to stop asking me if I was ready for this. Because the answer was no, I wasn't.

"Alright, Paul," Dad said with a fist in the air. "You got this."

Mom tilted her head like people did when they felt sorry for me. I had seen that look on her face too many times.

I stared at the ceiling as they rolled me out of the room and into the hallway, counting each passing light like one counts sheep before going to sleep. I was led through the double doors and into the operating room. I suddenly became aware of the sweaty palms of my hands. The room was noticeably cooler.

"Paul," said that cotton candy voice. I glanced at the needle she had in hand, watching as she inserted it into the tubing. "Count down from ten for me, okay?"

I nodded and started counting, "Ten, nine, eight, seven, six, fi…"

The animals painted on the walls sent a slight shiver down my body. They seemed to prance around, dancing to an annoying beeping sound. A cannula was stuck to the upper part of my left hand. A sharp pain crawled up my throat. The annoying tube was in it again. I would've sworn the thing was as wide as a silver dollar. Syringes pumped fluid into small tubes on both my arms. Two wider tubes filled with fluid crawled out from beneath the scar on my chest. There was also a stabbing pain underneath both my arms. More tubes—one on each side. Yes, Frankenstein had survived.

I searched the room for a familiar face, but it was empty except for me and the equipment keeping me alive. The sun waved goodbye as it set outside the window, hiding behind the mountains. I wanted to be the sun in that moment. I wanted to disappear and only return when all these wounds had healed. The heaven I had learned about sounded pretty darn nice right then.

Leaving this world meant more money for my parents; I was the kid draining most of it with medical bills. It also meant freedom from all the anxiety around Sawyer. Was he going to fail that day? Was he still beating normally? Was he giving out?

I'd welcome some relief from all the pain and torment. So would my family—even if they were reluctant to admit it. They wouldn't have to be anxious or worried. They would finally know the outcome.

The door opened slowly. It was the nurse from before. The hazel eyes gave her away before she said a word.

"You're awake already." She smiled. "I thought you were going to sleep some more. Your parents went home to freshen up, but I believe they'll be back today. You just went through a lot. You should rest."

There it was again. The look. Her eyes scanned my body like I was some lonely puppy waiting to be adopted. I looked away, the animal drawings on the wall suddenly becoming more interesting.

She turned on the TV and walked out of the room.

There was no escaping. That was it. That was my life.

Another Death

APRIL 2008

It had happened again. Less than one year after the death of our twins. Weeping was the soundtrack of our drive back from the hospital after the procedure. A few weeks ago, the gynecologist confirmed Olivia was pregnant again. And here we were, facing the unbearable pain of another miscarriage. Hearing the doctor confirm the lack of a heartbeat made the world implode inside me.

"It shouldn't be this difficult," Olivia kept repeating under her breath, clinging to the seat belt as if it were a lifeline that could take her back in time. "It shouldn't be this hard. It can't be."

She was always vocal about the life she wanted for us—and her words haunted me daily: a big family, a husband who worked in the mornings and came home late in the afternoons to spend time with them, a house surrounded by a white picket fence in the suburbs somewhere. The reality had become all too clear; I'd never be able to give her any of that. I was a defeated soldier on the battlefield of life, watching death after death drain our strength away.

We stopped at my parents' to pick up Neil. Olivia stayed in the car. They didn't ask many questions. As soon as Neil was buckled in, he started telling us about his day with Grandma while holding on to one of his dinosaurs.

"I found a worm on a tree," he said gleefully, waving the dinosaur around.

"You did?" Olivia sniffled, turning her head toward him, eyes puffed and red.

"Yes, and then I ate chocolate cake. It was so good. I also learned the name of a new dinosaur. Plo-plo-dicus."

"That's great, champ," I said, glancing at the rearview mirror. He probably meant Diplodocus but he looked too excited for me to correct him.

I reached for the radio, but Olivia grabbed my hand before I could turn it on.

"No, please. I need some peace and quiet."

"Dad," Neil started after a few minutes of silence.

"Yes?"

"Did Mom fall? Why is she crying?"

"Mom isn't feeling well," Olivia said. "But she'll get better soon."

"Okay," he answered, his attention shifting to his dinosaur.

The challenge of returning home after such an event was trying to find normalcy again. Neil paraded inside the house as soon as I opened the door, darting his way toward his toy basket in the corner of the living room. "Dad, let's play!" he insisted, spilling out his toys on the floor.

Olivia was about to walk up the stairs when Neil asked, "Mom, maybe playing will make it better?"

Olivia gave him a kiss on the forehead. "You're perfect, and Mom would love to play with you, but she needs to rest. Dad will take care of you. We can play tomorrow, okay?"

"Okay," Neil agreed and returned to his toys.

Olivia retreated to our bedroom. Her low sobs and whimpers carried quietly throughout the house for the rest of the day.

Dead Man Walking

JUNE 2008

"Our Love" filled my living room as I played. The tune had become an anchor for my sanity after my last visit to the doctor three days ago.

Sawyer—and my liver—were both enlarged. They had decided to gang up and put pressure on all my other organs. My right lung was on the verge of collapse. My protein levels were dangerously low. This was it. Sawyer had been wounded too much to be whole again.

Sawyer was sending messages that he was ready to shut down, but I didn't have the luxury to listen. I had to live for those around me.

Dr. Kupo prescribed an intravenous medication called Milrinone. The pump was placed in a fanny pack, a catheter inserted into a vein just below the bend in my elbow. I was lucky Olivia could change my dressings and manage the medication at home. Most patients had to be hospitalized.

They were going to adjust my medication and do a heart catherization in August to assess Sawyer's damage.

Dr. Kupo suggested we try cardioverting me again; a procedure that involves inducing you into a deep sleep and delivering an electric shockwave to the heart in an attempt to correct its beating pattern.

When I first experienced the procedure, the sleeping medicine didn't fully work. I thought my body was going to burst as the electric shock surged through my chest. It was like releasing fireworks inside a small bedroom. The second blow was even worse. I was a prisoner tied to an electric chair, robbed of every ability save one—pain.

Olivia and Neil were in the living room surrounded by action figures, cars, and building blocks. I watched them while I played, thinking about the human bomb they had with them. I was about to explode, and the carnage would hurt them the most.

Dad told me he had heard my voice in the wind after my first surgery. That's how he knew I was going to be alright. But I was an adult and Sawyer was still sick. Maybe this was the end. I had grown up and finally arrived at the finish line.

Yes, I was confident in a beautiful and mysterious afterlife, but I was too stubborn to leave this world behind. I *literally* didn't have the heart to cause my loved ones so much pain. I was a boxer, prepped and ready to fight off death itself for my family.

When Olivia struggled with doubts and I got knocked down, I was going to keep getting up and going another round. If my son was at risk of living without a father, I was going to cling to life with all I had. And if I was to depart this world, I wanted them to remember me, not as a man who was defeated by his heart, but as the man who fought wholeheartedly until the end.

The Choice

AUGUST 2008

I couldn't breathe. Had someone put a bag over my head? Sawyer, even in declining health, could still give me painful thuds. With heavy-lidded eyes, I spotted silhouettes all around me. I tried crying for help, but my mouth was a locked chest.

Was this it?

Olivia's face flooded my mind. I had to see her smile one more time. There was so much I still wanted to say. There was so much I wanted us to live for. Neil's face followed. I couldn't leave him. I had to see him grow up.

While struggling to fight against whatever had a grip on me, everything faded away into nothing. The darkness in my mind was replaced with some sort of dream.

I was in a fetal position on the ground. Women in long white garments stood around me, weeping. Their wailing was accompanied by rolling thunder. I cried for help but suddenly realized what was in front of me. How could I have not seen it? A cross was an arm's length away. The uneven patterns of its wooden base led my gaze upward, until I felt something dripping on my shoulder. Blood.

Another drip.

I chanced a look, following its source. There was a man hanging on the cross. His arms were spread, hands nailed to the wood. One foot was on top of the other, nailed together, and on his head was a crown of thorns. The image in front of me blurred as I squinted, hoping to see the face of the man.

But I didn't need a face. I knew who He was.

That's when I remembered something. Scholars had affirmed those crucified like Jesus eventually died of suffocation. The weight of the victim's torso became too much for the ribs and collarbone to withstand. The lungs were crushed. The only brief relief for the victim was to stand on the platform below their nailed feet to take a breath.

I decided to stand on my platform and breathe despite my nailed feet. I had to stick around for those around me. I couldn't leave this world. Not yet.

Muffled voices joined the irritating, yet familiar, beeping sound. My eyes opened, landing on the diaper commercial playing on TV. Olivia was to my left, sitting on a leather chair and wrapped in a brown sweater.

"Hey, you," I said in a croaked voice.

She jumped up, startled.

"How are you feeling?" She rushed closer and kissed my forehead.

"I'm good—better now."

"Glad to hear." She chuckled. "You slept for twelve hours."

"Wait, what happened?" I asked, confused.

"You underwent the heart catherization procedure yesterday, remember? They've been waiting for you to wake up to let us know how the procedure went," she said with a smile. "You're still here, so I guess it went well."

I almost told her what I had seen, but decided to keep it to myself. The revelation felt so powerful and private that I couldn't share it with anyone, regardless of how much I loved them. She stroked my hair and said, "I'm going to tell them you're awake. Let's see what they have to say."

She returned moments later, followed by Dr. Kupo.

"Hey there, Paul," he said, clipboard in hand. Olivia sat on the edge of my bed. "How are you feeling?" He fixed his thick-framed glasses over his nose. His graying gelled hair glistened under the light.

"Good." I cleared my throat. "Am I going to still be good after I hear what you have to say?"

He chuckled and flipped a page on his clipboard. "Well,

the good news is your pacemaker and the amiodarone therapy have steadied your heart rhythm, buying you some more time." His words lifted a weight from my shoulders. "But"—the weight returned—"we're concerned about the right side of your heart. It's literally become a balloon, and blood just swirls inside. Picture a whole bunch of cars on a roundabout driving without a clear exit. A Fontan revision should help with that."

"Fontan," I whispered. "The same surgery I had when I was fourteen?"

"Yes. But more advanced."

"I should be alright after that?" I asked. Olivia's face was shrouded in concern.

He paused. "Well, if the revision works, you should be fine for a while. If not, we'll look at alternatives." His lips flattened into a line as the tension thickened. "There's no easy way for me to say this. Your heart is failing, Paul. Though I am not fond of the idea, my advice would be to start meeting with the transplant team as a final resort in case this doesn't work." He removed his glasses.

Not fond of the idea. Final resort. The words whirled in my head as if they had been screamed into an empty cave. I wanted to ask him what that meant, but I was scared of the answer.

Mustering up the courage, I asked, "What do you mean by final resort?" My brows pulled together. "I thought, when the time came, a transplant would solve all this."

"I need to be honest with you," he said, face deadpan. "There's a strong chance a transplant will kill you at this point." The certainty in his voice confirmed my fear. "Your liver is too damaged. It's been pushed too far and is barely breaking down any protein. The Fontan revision is your best option. And I recommend you start wearing your oxygen tubing full-time."

"And what happens after the Fontan?" I asked.

"One step at a time. But the choice is ultimately yours."

Olivia's eyes were two dark chasms.

"I'll have them bring you some food," Dr. Kupo said amidst the lingering silence. "I know you must be hungry. You slept through breakfast."

"Thank you." I stared into the distance.

I got a brand-new oxygen concentrator after I was sent home. I called it R2D2. It was bulky and white with four wheels that allowed me to drag it around the house like a leashed dog. It beeped like a microwave whenever I turned it on. R2D2 was so state-of-the-art it even had room for a humidifier bottle. Seeing my oxygen tube connected to it reminded me I had no way out of this. The transplant—the one thing I thought would save my life—was also the blade that could take it all away.

A few days later, I was struck with the news that my health insurance no longer covered my procedures due to major healthcare changes happening in the United States. I applied for a new government program offering those with pre-existing conditions some relief. The good news was I got even better insurance. The bad news was that I had to leave Dr. Kupo's care.

I was referred a new congenital cardiologist named Angie Brown. Olivia told me she was the doctor at Primary Children's Hospital—the same hospital where I had my Fontan when I was fourteen. When I asked why I was being referred to a doctor there, I was told most people in my condition didn't survive past childhood. I was one of the few.

On a Monday morning, while working on some music for the new album, I decided to call Dr. Brown with the number provided by my new insurance. To no surprise, I was sent to voicemail. I put my phone on the music rack and lost myself in an improv until my phone vibrated a few minutes later. The caller ID displayed an unknown number.

"This is Dr. Brown. I just got your voicemail." The voice was mellow and calm.

Sawyer pounded at her words. "Thank you for calling me back, Doctor. I would've expected one of your assistants to reach out so I could schedule an appointment."

"I wanted to personally talk to you. It's not exactly protocol to be personal, but I enjoy your music and your case is fascinating." I glanced down at the piano while she spoke, catching my reflection on the black glossy surface. "How are you feeling?"

"I'll be honest." I sighed. "I am really hoping you *can* help me."

I shared Dr. Kupo's diagnosis. Every word coming out of me squeezed the vise around Sawyer tighter.

"Paul," she said as soon as I was done. "I'm not sure what on earth those people are thinking. You need a transplant! The Fontan revision will kill you." Her voice was as sharp as steel.

"What do you mean?"

"A healthy heart should help your liver break down protein," she explained. "The oxygen flow from a new heart would heal your liver. The revision won't."

Silence.

"Can you come in for a few tests tomorrow afternoon? I need to check your heart and liver."

"I think so," I replied. "My wife will be home. She might be able to drive me."

"Perfect. Can you come at two?"

"Yes. I'll call if anything changes."

"See you then," she said, followed by the dial tone.

My eyes followed the oxygen tube connecting me to R2D2. It was to my left, snuggled up against the wall beside my piano bench. The buttons and lights on its surface mimicked staring eyes. I didn't want to spend the rest of my life plugged into a machine. And it sounded like my best chance at freedom was to risk the wisp of life I still had left.

Olivia drove me to the hospital the next day—along with another version of my oxygen machine. It was the portable model that got to leave the house with me. It had two wheels and two metal legs that stretched outward. The top of the silver cylinder was green, serving as support for the regulator, pressure valve, and flow meter. From it stemmed a metal handle, its tip warped into a black handlebar. I had it between my legs in the front seat.

I lost my breath when I spotted the white letters spelling *Primary Children's Hospital.* They were suspended above three round columns, surrounded by tinted glass windows.

Here we are again, I thought.

Olivia helped me with my oxygen cylinder as I stepped out of the car. Walking through the doors wheeling my oxygen source actually made Sawyer skip a beat.

The front desk was the same as it was twenty years ago, with the exception of a few crayon drawings hanging on its edge. The painted mural on the wall behind it depicted children playing in a park; it looked like some of its colors had been retouched throughout the years. My eyes scanned the drawing, catching on the girl sporting a yellow shirt and a wide smile. She reminded me of someone I hadn't thought of in a long time, a fellow patient and faithful companion during my recovery after the Fontan. She would visit me every single day, and her presence was one of the few joys I had while cooped up. Her name was Stephanie.

Being back was like walking into a distant nightmare.

We were led to Dr. Brown's office a few minutes after we arrived. I stared at the canvas behind her desk and took a seat as we waited. It displayed a brown moth with its wings spread out, the two circles on their surface giving the impression the creature had eyes there.

Olivia observed the moth as well, face rigid. I laid a hand on hers and said, "It'll be alright."

She replied with a halfhearted smile.

Dr. Brown walked in, fixing her white coat as she rounded her desk.

"It's a pleasure meeting you in person," she said as Olivia and I stood to greet her. "I have a good feeling about this." She shook my hand.

"At least one of us does," I said behind a sigh and pointed to Olivia. "This is my wife, Olivia."

"Pleasure." She shook her hand and took a seat. "Sorry it took me a while. I have to say, I'm glad your medical file is now on the computer. It's pretty long." She smiled.

"The bible of all medical files," I joked.

She highlighted a few facts that stood out to her. My heart being enlarged. My right lung being crushed. My liver failing. She insisted the transplant was the safest option. She analyzed my face after she was done presenting the facts that supported her claim. I picked up on her quick glance at the oxygen tube connected to the cylinder next to me. She crossed her hands on the table. "I'm going to request a few x-rays and ultrasounds today. The tests should confirm my theory."

"You do realize the weight this puts on our family, right?" Olivia's face remained rigid. "His old doctor says one thing. You're saying another."

"Well, eventually a decision needs to be made," said Dr. Brown. "I'm his doctor now. And from everything you said, he needs a fresh reboot. I do want to wait for the test results so we can be completely sure, but I stand by what I said."

Olivia and I exchanged a glance.

"Can I make a decision after the test results?" I asked.

"Absolutely. Let me go speak to the nurse so we can get everything ready."

She exited the room. I followed the patterns on the outstretched wings of the moth. I knew they didn't pose a threat, but I bet all moths secretly wished to be butterflies.

Dr. Brown returned and asked me to follow her, informing Olivia we'd be back in about half an hour.

She led me to another private room where I was left with an EKG machine and an ultrasound tech. I was familiar with the equipment. It could show how fast—or slow—my heart was beating. But one thing I was never going to get used to was taking off my shirt in front of them. The aftermath of all my medical procedures had turned me into a broken gallery. Aside from the scar collection, my shoulders had turned inward, and my chest sunk in a bit. I'd always joke with my techs, saying I was actually a centerfold model and had the staples to prove it.

The tech applied pads to my skin that connected to the wires spilling out of the computer. They ran several tests before I was led back to Olivia. I was told to come back the next day for the results.

We returned as requested. The picture of the moth held my attention until Dr. Brown entered the room. Sawyer pounded faster and faster as she walked to her seat. He seemed to be trying to beat at the pace of her steps. Olivia was nervous, every noise and murmur seemed to put her on edge.

"I have good news," Dr. Brown revealed. "The results came back, and everything points to the transplant being your best option. Like I mentioned before, a healthy four-chamber heart will fully restore liver function and strengthen any organs struggling to keep up. It might be a risky procedure, but there's a good chance of it working out."

Olivia smiled. "So, he'll make it?"

"Mrs. Cardall, I can't downplay the risks. The amount of scar tissue that has built up over the years will make it challenging. But the odds of the transplant are much better than those of the Fontan." She cleared her throat and turned to me. "And there's something else; testing did confirm your liver is worse. If we don't get that liver healthy, the chances of you living without a transplant are slim."

Olivia took in a sharp breath. "The choice is yours, Paul."

I locked eyes with the two circles on the wings of the moth. "The transplant it is."

After meeting with Dr. Brown and the transplant team on August 22, I received my pager and was listed as a recipient.

Doctors always talked about getting listed for a transplant as something hopeful. And it was. But you don't really think about it until you're in those shoes. Thousands wait for their chance at a new heart.

I was to take a sabbatical from traveling outside of Salt Lake City since the call could come in at any moment. They explained the pager could go off within the next two months up to a whole year. But once it did, I had a one-hour window to get to the hospital. I was also instructed to avoid as much human interaction as possible because another infection could end my life.

I started journaling my experience on my computer while waiting for a heart. I wanted Neil to know the story from my perspective, in case I left this world when Sawyer did. But with each entry, I thought about the millions of people who had no idea what waiting for a heart actually meant. I had something in my hands—an experience that could inspire so many. The words Mrs. Dominguez spoke to me the day I almost fainted at school came back to me, *"Take control of your story. Tell it in your own words. The world will never be able to rip it away after you do."*

I felt like it was my duty to share the ups and downs of the coming months—or years—with the world. I already had an audience, and they had the power to snowball this whole thing. They knew my music, but I wanted them to know my story as well.

I decided to take my entries and post them on a blog. I consulted with Olivia before uploading the first one. She was reluctant, claiming she didn't want our lives and family exposed to strangers. She also pointed out that making this public could potentially expose the donor of my new heart—when I eventually had one. I proceeded to make the account public despite her concerns,. *She'll eventually understand,* I thought.

An Unexpected Visitor

AUGUST 1987

My temporary address became the Pediatric Intensive Care Unit inside the Primary Children's Hospital. After my Fontan procedure, I couldn't help but picture a massive fountain gushing out blood instead of water whenever they discussed it with me. I eventually learned it was named after the guy who invented it, Francis Fontan.

My hope of leaving after a few days was dashed when they told me the pacemaker they installed in my chest didn't work properly. The culprit: Sawyer's anatomy. The result: They had to pry me open again and move the pacemaker to my abdomen. Sawyer lacked the proper veins to thread the pacemaker's wires—or leads—into place. The leads are responsible for delivering energy to the heart so it can keep beating. By moving it to my chest, they could transfer the electrical signal through the outer walls of Sawyer's muscles. They were held in place by literally screwing the leads into the heart. Fun stuff.

The day before surgery was a nerve fest. I didn't want them

to open me up again. But it wasn't like I had a choice. The scar on my chest was doomed to become a secret passageway doctors would use to reach Sawyer whenever he needed fixing. The future held so many more operations. I was only fourteen and was already tired of it.

They wheeled me back to the operating room. I knew pain waited for me, no matter the outcome. Whole-body pain that I knew well.

The bright lights above my head blinded me once I was on the operating table. I hated the temperature of the room, the little breeze from the air conditioning that sent a shiver down my spine. I hated the smell of iodine, flooding my senses from the freshly cleaned surface beneath me. The surgical team moved around quickly and knowingly as they prepared to open me up. None of them cared, or had time to hear, that I was terrified. I prayed in silence, words only God could hear. I wished for relief. Whether it came from death or Sawyer's improvement, I didn't care. I just wanted somewhat of a normal life.

The animals on the walls of my room had begun to feel like my pets. Seeing them whenever I awoke from surgery meant Sawyer had been a good boy. The clock on the wall marked the time: 6:15 a.m.

My parents walked in a few minutes later. Mom's cheeks were puffed and red, matching the scarlet sweater she wore. Dad had his hands folded behind his back, chin high, face rigid.

"How are you feeling?" Mom's chin trembled.

"I'm alright," I said weakly. "Tired." A groan. "Everything okay?"

They exchanged a worried glance.

"Paul," Dad said and paused. "The doctor was speaking to your mother and me."

My stomach churned. He seemed to be looking for the right words to break some bad news.

"Just say it, Dad. What is it?"

"One of the leads from your pacemaker fell off your heart while you were asleep." He kept his eyes on me, probably trying to hide the fact he'd rather stare at the wall than at his son while breaking the news. "They're going to have to operate on you again."

My attention was on the window by my bed. An orange hue peeked out amidst the dark clouds in the sky, slowly revealing the mountaintops of Olympus on the horizon. Despair crashed like a tsunami; the first wave fools you into thinking things won't be so bad but, in the blink of an eye, there's a second, a third, and then you're drowning.

"I'm done," I mumbled as the dawn blurred behind my tears. "I'm tired. I'd rather die than live like this." My gaze met theirs. "Tell God to take me away from this life. Whatever that means. Please."

If Sawyer had a throat, seeing my parents' suffering would be the hand that choked it. Mom tried to hold back her tears, but they eventually escaped. Dad's frown remained intact, as if every wrinkle had a word to say. Determination suddenly replaced his sorrow. He sniffled and folded his arms like he always did when he was about to reprimand me.

"Paul, you'll live a long life." A smile. "You'll see. And somehow, all of this will be for the greater good. Stop asking God to end a season you don't understand yet. It'll all make sense. Let science and the divine help you live."

I listened to my Dad, not because it was what I wanted to hear, but due to the sheer amount of strength it must have taken in that moment to discipline me and shift my perspective. Seeing your kid in the situation I was in must be terrible.

My dad's words were my anchor when the nurses showed up to wheel me back to the operating table.

The time was 6:45 a.m. I took in a breath to make sure I wasn't dreaming. No, I wasn't. I was about to press the button to call the nurse but was startled by a little girl standing next to my bed.

She had a sweet smile stretching from ear to ear on her pale face and hair down to her shoulders. She couldn't have been more than nine. I wasn't sure if she stared with compassion or curiosity. Maybe she thought I was winning the tubes-coming-out-of-our-bodies contest. Mine flowed out of my mouth and torso like snaking rivers while her single tube spilled out of a hole in her neck.

She waved with a shy smile. I waved back. The tube in my trachea triggered a sharp pain as I attempted to smile. I scowled as my muscles went rigid. She laid a hand on my arm, probably noticing my struggle.

Our eyes locked. Dark circles spread around hers. We stared at each other as if our silence could offer up answers to our questions. What was her story? How did she end up here?

She left the room when one of the nurses came in to check on me. But her visits became a daily habit. I got to speak to her after my tube was removed. I was the only one to experience that relief. She still couldn't get a word out because of the hole in her neck. She'd bring a whiteboard and marker to draw or try to write what she wanted to say.

I looked forward to seeing her every day. Her visits made me feel like I had someone that understood my struggle. Her mom came to my room with her one day. That was when I learned her name was Stephanie. They looked alike, sharing the same round green eyes and blonde hair. Her mom's name was Patsy. She carried an envelope on the day she visited. Stephanie watched eagerly as her mom handed it to me. She grasped the bar handles of my bed, resting her chin on them, staring at me like I was a movie theater screen. The gesture was my signal to open the envelope immediately. Inside was a drawing of a girl in green scrubs lying on a bed covered with colorful flowers under a tree. The girl was comprised of a collection of sticks drawn with crayons, the yellow coloring her hair bleeding over her round face. My fingers trailed over the drawing.

Stephanie pointed at the girl on the paper and at herself.

"She wants you to know that's her," Patsy said. "She spent a few hours working on this."

"I love it," I said, my words stinging my throat—the pain a keepsake from the tube that had been lodged there. "It's beautiful." Maybe the emotion I could see leaking onto the page was her longing for paradise and relief. I studied her eager expression, wondering why I got to recover faster than she did. She was doomed to keep on wearing that thing in her neck like an unwanted accessory. While my scars were concealed, hers were out in the open. As the days dragged on, my tubes were removed while hers remained.

She came to see me on my last day at the hospital, her sadness on full display. She wore a bright yellow shirt with a rainbow across the chest.

"Can I get a smile?" I asked, sitting on the edge of my bed in my blue jeans, my favorite white shirt Mom brought from home, and my Vans. She forced one, carrying a mixture of happiness and loss. "I'm going home today." A clap followed my words. "And I can't wait for the day when it's your turn to go home."

Her mouth trembled, struggling to say something. A breath was all she could manage. Frustration covered her face. She took a step back.

"Hey, we'll see each other again," I declared. "You're going to leave this place and have an incredible life. It'll be great."

"Stephanie!" Mom emerged from the hallway. They had met a few days before. "I'm happy to see you here. Did you come to say bye to Paul?"

Stephanie nodded.

"That's great, sweetheart." Mom knelt in front of her. "Listen, when you leave, I want you to come to the house for dinner. How does that sound?" Excitement filled Stephanie's face. "Good. We'll see you soon, okay?"

Mom grabbed my bag and led me out of the room. I looked over my shoulder while walking down the hall. Stephanie waved at me, then stood rooted to her spot by the door until Mom and I walked through the double doors leading to the elevator.

As we crossed the lobby, I noticed a few artists painting a mural behind the front desk. The outline depicted a scene of children playing in a park, half of it already painted in bright colors.

As Mom and I walked toward the exit, I wondered if Stephanie would ever get the chance to play outside. Had her voice whispered to her parents that everything would be alright? Would she grow old?

A Light in the Dark

OCTOBER 1987

I sat on the floor of my bedroom, legs crossed, back pressed against the foot of my bed, and an Indiana Jones novel in hand. Jonahs was on his bed flipping through a geology book he got from a friend. Recovery was going well, the pacemaker clearly working since my fingers and lips were no longer blue.

Stephanie's face would enter my mind every so often throughout the day. And I'd dream of her every other night. She'd wave at me from my bedside, her smile a faint line. I couldn't wait to see her again and hoped that tube would be gone by then. Even Jonahs was looking forward to meeting her whenever she was able to visit.

Dan barged into the room and plopped on his bed. "Paul, Mom wants you," he said, beginning to flip through the pages of a comic book.

"Everything okay?" My eyes remained on the yellowed pages of my book.

"Didn't ask. I'm more concerned about Superman at the moment."

I tossed the worn-out copy on the floor and grasped the foot of the bed to stand. Jonahs immediately leapt from his bed and put his shoulder under my arm, helping me to my feet. Dan lifted his eyes from the comic book to observe.

"I'm okay," I said with a chuckle. "I promise you."

"Just making sure," he said.

There was this sense of achievement every time I managed to walk up the steps into the kitchen without my lungs begging for air.

My parents were putting the groceries away.

"Need any help?" I asked.

"No, honey," Mom said, stowing a few cans of soup in the pantry. "Just take a seat."

I pulled a stool out and sat by the counter, the kitchen illuminated by the rays of the setting sun.

Mom wiped her hands on a cloth by the stove and sat next to me. Dad reclined on the counter, arms folded.

"Your dad and I saw Patsy at the market," she said, holding my hand. "Stephanie died, sweetie."

I jerked my hand away. "What do you mean?"

"We grabbed lunch after we saw each other at the store," Dad said. "She told us she died a few days after you left."

"No, no, no," I mumbled. "How? I mean…"

"She had an unusual case of cystic fibrosis," Dad answered.

I had heard about cystic fibrosis before. The disease slowly destroys the lungs and digestive system. In my head, I imagined a beast crawling around inside her body, eating her organs away.

"I get that she was really sick, but she should have lived longer, right?" I asked, hoping to find reason. "She should have had the chance to leave that hospital too. This is so unfair."

"I'm sorry," Mom said. "There aren't explanations for situations like these. That doesn't mean we won't get to understand them in the future. God—"

"God," I scoffed. "Oh, I believe in Him, alright. But why do some get their miracle while others don't?"

"All eventually get their miracle," Dad said. "Some in this world. Others in the next."

"And what are we supposed to learn from all this?" I barked.

"Paul." Mom's voice was like a warm blanket. "Time can be a great teacher. You may not see it now. You may not even understand what I'm about to say. But pain gives us wisdom. It numbs us to the things that don't truly matter."

I tried to keep it from rolling away, but a tear escaped the corner of my eye.

"Her mom said your company kept her alive a little longer." Dad's words hurt Sawyer and me both. "Doctors kept telling her not to wander down the halls so she could save her strength." He forced a sad smile. "But they were amazed that she kept hanging on. Maybe she held on a little longer because she kept visiting you."

"She told her mom you were the star that made her darkness a little brighter," Mom said. "Maybe you provided more joy in those few days than she had in her lifetime. You were her friend at the end."

"Her friend," I groaned, defeated.

"We're so sorry." Mom wiped the tear rolling down my cheek with a finger. "We wish we could keep you safe from the world. But sorrow is a part of life." She sighed. "We're here if you need to talk."

"There's not much to say, is there? I'm going—I'm going for a walk."

"Paul," Dad said. "It'll be alright."

How do you know, Dad? You've never had someone cut you open to fix your brokenness. You've never had to live the life I do. Yes, we all expect death at some point, but I hear its whispers every single day. I don't remember you ever having to call a hospital home. I don't need sympathy from healthy people.

I darted into my room.

"You okay?" Jonahs stared at me like he'd seen a ghost.

Dan's eyes followed me.

I opened the drawer of the nightstand and grabbed my Walkman.

Jonahs dropped the book on his bed and sat up. "You want—"

"Not now, Jonahs!"

I grabbed a sweatshirt from the closet, walked upstairs, and went outside. My ability to breathe perfectly made me angrier. I got my so-called miracle. She didn't.

The crisp fall air brushed my cheeks as I wandered down the street, observing the sun setting behind Mount Olympus. I pressed play on my Walkman, ready to embrace whatever song played from the mix tape I made when I came home from the hospital. Ironically, the cassette began playing "How Soon Is Now?" by The Smiths.

Stephanie kept visiting some broken boy, wasting her energy when she could've stayed in bed conserving her strength. That's all I kept thinking.

I walked aimlessly, as if my walking could bring her back. But as darkness crawled across the sky, I realized she had become like the sun, setting on this world to rise on the next. Only there had been no afternoon to warn anyone that Stephanie's sun was about to set.

The days that followed were filled with questions—the majority without any logical answers. What was life's criteria for choosing those who lived and died? Death had been a close friend of mine since birth, yet, despite our closeness, never picked me.

What was it? What did I have that made me go on? I was

sure God heard my thoughts of death and how I was ready for it. I'd been praying to God ever since my parents taught me. And yet, still, it skipped me. Sawyer must've also been tired of being cut and bruised by doctors. Why hadn't the bastard just quit yet?

It had been two weeks since she died. I went to bed earlier than usual. Dan and Jonahs were engrossed in some cartoon in the living room, but I wanted to be alone with the image of her face. Somehow, seeing her in my head eased my guilt of being alive. But Jonahs interrupted me. He entered the room a few minutes after I was under the covers.

"You alright?" He stood by the foot of my bed in dinosaur pajamas.

"You keep asking me that," I replied, eyes on the ceiling and hands crossed over my chest.

"It wasn't your fault." His words surprised me. "You don't think I haven't noticed you lately? Ever since Mom told you about Stephanie, it's like you feel guilty for every breath you take. You're punishing yourself for something you didn't do."

I shrugged. "I don't know what to feel. I just keep wondering why."

"Maybe she stuck around a little longer so you could live,"

he said. "She decided to spend whatever energy she had left to make you smile."

"That's an unfair thing to say."

"Is it?" He sat on my bed. "Is it unfair to help someone else in need? Someone like you?"

"When it costs their life? Yes."

"But if we don't live to help each other, then what's the point? What if you gave her life more meaning? Did you think about that?" He scratched the back of his uncombed head of hair.

"Do we ever get to ask life anything?" I asked, my back now pressed against the headboard. "Or do we just go along with whatever it throws our way?"

"We can ask for the wisdom to live it. And the courage to understand it."

I stared at my ten-year-old brother and wondered where he got all that from.

"If you feel guilty, you erase all the good she did for you. You're practically putting her in a box of suffering. We all have a version of paradise. Maybe you were the paradise that gave her a few extra days on this Earth." His gaze shifted to the ground. "Maybe you're here because of her. Maybe I have you next to me because of her."

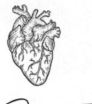

All I See Is Snow

DECEMBER 2008

"Jingle Blels, Jingle Blels," Neil sang around the house as if performing at a concert. He wore a red bow tie and suspenders over a white shirt with Christmas trees all over it.

I watched my favorite entertainer from the couch while waiting for Olivia. My portable oxygen cylinder was already blowing air up my nose. Around my waste was the fanny pack containing my dosage of Milrinone. A tube stemmed from the right side and snaked up my shirt and out the sleeve, pumping medicine into the artery on my right arm. It was taped to my skin so it wouldn't be jerked away by accident. This was the most comfortable I could be while leaving the house since receiving the pager—which had already become obsolete. Since the majority of people had cellphones, the pager program faded.

I was looking forward to spending Christmas Eve at my parents'. Truth be told, I couldn't wait to spend a few hours beyond the walls of my home. It was worth the risk. Such moments had become a rare occasion. I had barely seen my parents since August. Mom also told me Jonahs was finally coming, his first time visiting since he moved to Arizona.

Thankfully, inspiration didn't need a healthy body to thrive. I kept composing. I'd wake up, and the first thing I'd do was go to the piano. I'd shut my eyes and escape to a place in my mind where my body was healthy and my heart strong. But when the melodies ceased, reality remained, and the tubes inserted into my body reminded me of the truth.

I had released two projects that year: *Living for Eden* and *The Hymns Collection.* I needed to keep the money coming in due to the extra medical expenses not covered by my insurance. I even had another release scheduled for next year entitled *Sacred Piano.* The music would also be a source of income for Olivia and Neil in case I didn't make it.

"Neil, you're going to puke if you keep doing that!" I said, watching him spin while singing "Jingle Blels."

There were three oxygen cylinders lined up against the wall next to the stairs. They were also coming with us in case I needed an extra boost. Neil's reflection graced their metal surfaces as he kept on spinning and singing.

My son's unblemished joy was the canvas, paint, and brush my mind needed to create a picture of Stephanie from all those years ago. Her big eyes and the tube—that damn tube—spilling out of her throat. My fingers followed the oxygen tubes on my face as I remembered the sound of her footsteps filling my hospital room whenever she visited. She spent the energy she had left on a broken boy with a broken heart. I was ready to do the same for my family. Even if the call never came.

"Ready to go?" Olivia walked into the living room, wearing a black dress down to her knees and a red belt with a bow around the waist. She was in flats, hair tied up, her perfume as sweet as her smile.

"You're going to freeze in that dress," I said, standing up.

"I'll be fine." She handed over my coat. "It's a five-second walk to the car and a five-second walk to your parents' house."

I waited by the door as Olivia carried the cylinders outside. It was ironic that the oxygen doctors prescribed for people who struggled to breathe came in containers that weighed about twenty pounds each. I had to watch my wife carry them through the snow, feeling like I couldn't carry my own weight.

We could hear the whole family from the driveway, the sounds of laughter, chatter, and Christmas music spilling out of the house. The front yard was a Christmas wonderland; six reindeer were positioned on one side, their heads bobbing up and down. The tree on the opposite side was wrapped in golden lights, fake gifts placed at its base. And the wreath on the door was wrapped in multicolored lights.

A joyful roar erupted once we walked inside. Mom rushed our way, greeted us, and scooped up Neil, taking him to the living room where he joined his cousin Zoe. I couldn't believe Jonahs and Hannah's daughter was almost two. Where had the time gone?

My parents went overboard on the decorations again. There was a Christmas arrangement on every piece of furniture. Santas, reindeer, elves, and snowmen hung on every wall. The house smelled of cookies, chocolate, and freshly baked banana bread.

I suddenly became very aware of the tube in my arm as Olivia helped me remove my coat. It prickled at my skin but thankfully remained in place. I looked for Jonahs and Hannah, but they were nowhere in sight.

I dragged my oxygen cylinder to the couch near the kitchen window. I knew Mount Olympus was out there, hidden by the night.

The Christmas tree was on the opposite side of the couch. Silver and red decorations clung to the pine swaddled in lights and icicles.

I scanned everyone's faces, listened to their laughter, and wondered if I'd be back next year. As I wheezed, my attention shifted to the door leading down to the basement. I shuddered at the memory of almost passing out on those stairs. And there I was again, lungs crawling for breath, Sawyer begging for life, and my body slowly turning to skin and bone.

Footsteps startled me. They were followed by laughter. Jonahs and Hannah emerged from the basement dressed in ugly Christmas sweaters. Hannah's was bright red, crowded with candy canes and reindeer. Jonahs' sweater was blue, its pattern a collection of Santas dressed in beach clothes. Jonahs' smile dimmed when he saw me. He remained still as the color drained from his face.

"Paul!" Hannah walked toward me, clearly trying to break the awkward tension. "How are you? It's been a while."

"I'm great," I replied in a raspy voice. "According to Neil, I look like Pinocchio with all the strings attached."

"Hey, if that's what it takes to keep you alive, Paulie." Her eyes darted over her shoulder.

Jonahs stood a few feet back, eyes glazed over and staring into the distance, head twitching.

"Hey, man," I said. "Going to say hello? I haven't heard from you in forever. So, what, you move to Arizona and forget your brother?"

"Yeah, yeah." He snapped out of his daze, trudging toward me with shuddering breaths. "Been...just been busy. Things are a little crazy with Zoe and things..."

He'd try to look at me, but he just couldn't.

"It's good to see you," I said.

"Good to see you," he whispered. "Yeah, it's good. But shouldn't you be home? Mom said you were going to be home."

Hannah scowled and laced her fingers with his.

"It's Christmas," I said, confused. "Why would I stay home?"

"Got to stay healthy," he mumbled. "For your new heart, right? Too many people here, no?"

They retreated to the living room before I had the chance to say anything. Mom stared at me from a distance before making her way over.

"Everything okay?" she asked.

"You told Jonahs I wasn't going to be here." I frowned. "Why?"

She took in a worried breath. "Hannah…she…said he's been acting strange since we told him about the transplant."

"So you had to tell him I wouldn't be here?"

"She said he's been very anxious about your situation, Paul." She sat on the armrest of the couch. "Your brother is just worried." A brief silence. "And his diagnosis didn't help. I figured this would make it easier. If he saw you."

"What diagnosis are you talking about?" Our eyes locked, hers filled with sadness.

"Your brother saw a few doctors over the summer. One diagnosed him as bipolar, and the other said he has severe anxiety.

We're just trying to avoid things that might trigger him right now."

"And none of you thought about telling me that?" I asked.

"How could we add more weight to your shoulders? I knew if I told you, you'd stay home, but God knows how long you—" An exasperated breath was all she managed.

I remained rooted to the couch as Mom rejoined the family. Neil, Zoe, and the other cousins were inseparable. Jonahs remained aloof. Hannah would glance at me here and there. I didn't need to say anything; she knew I was aware of what was happening to my brother.

At one point in the night, the family gathered to watch the kids do a play of the nativity scene. They had costumes, a manger, and a Cabbage Patch doll that was supposed to be baby Jesus. We were all in a circle in the living room so the kids had enough space to act out their scenes. The couch by the window was my VIP seat. Olivia eventually joined me. While Dad narrated the story, Joseph lost his fake beard, Mary tripped on the train of her robe, and Cabbage Patch Jesus got knocked off the manger by one of the cousins dressed like a lamb. It was an adorably bad skit.

Dinner followed their hilarious enactment. Everyone ate, drank, and talked. I tried to get in the spirit but kept noticing that Jonahs didn't engage at all. He excused himself from the table and didn't come back.

I stood in the doorway looking down into the dark basement, the sounds of mutters and whimpers just barely reaching my ears. I held on to the wooden rail, picked up my oxygen tank, and started my climb down. Step by step. Breath by breath. Whenever I lost my balance, I pressed my shoulder against the wall, closed my eyes, and counted to ten before continuing.

The whimpers evolved into painful moans as I approached the bottom of the stairs. The door to our room was slightly open, the only source of light the glow of the Christmas lights coming through the window.

Jonahs lay on the bed, face buried in a pillow, arms wrapped around the Jesus Cabbage Patch doll. Sawyer quickened his pace as I approached him.

"Jonahs," I whispered. "Are you okay?"

"I need Him," he croaked. "I need Him. He needs to help me."

"Need who?" My fingers tingled as I touched his shoulder.

"Jesus." He sniffled. "He needs to calm my storm."

"Jonahs, you're alright." I sat next to him.

"You don't know!" he barked, head jolting up from the pillow. His eyes bulged out of their sockets, the veins in his neck visible even in the dim light. "I just want to be alone with Him."

I had never seen my brother like that. The smart, tender man was replaced by a stranger. He wept, holding on to that doll as if it could save his life. He calmed down after a while, loosening his grip around it.

He slowly stood to his feet, wiping his tears with his wrists. He scanned the room, confused. He spread his fingers and brought them to eye level, surveying his arms, body, and then my face.

"What happened?" he asked.

My mind raced for the best way to answer.

"Did it happen again?" He tossed the Cabbage Patch doll on the bed.

Silence.

"Paul?" he insisted.

"Everything will be alright," I said.

He sat beside me on the end of the bed, elbows on his knees. "What's wrong with me? What's..." Sobs followed.

I placed an arm around his shoulder and listened to his pain. His weeping was a sad song, the low notes so familiar to me. I wanted to ask him a thousand questions.

"We should go back to the party," I suggested after a few minutes. "People are going to come looking for us soon. Think you can handle it?"

"I guess." He sniffled. "Oh, man, this is messed up. I'm so messed up."

"Don't think that way. Listen, we'll figure it out. Just focus on tonight. We're here as a family, together. Everyone loves you. I'm glad I was the one to find you."

His tongue trailed over his lips. "I saw a few doctors a while ago."

"Mom told me," I said.

"I didn't want to worry you. You have a lot to think about. They have me on some pill. They say it's just a precaution, but the episodes are becoming more constant." He frowned. "Sorry I didn't tell you. You have so much going on already."

"I'm glad you did. Just take care of yourself, okay?"

"I'll try." A discouraged smile followed his words. "And you just remain strong until you find that new heart. Zoe needs her uncle."

"I'll try," I repeated.

"This will make sense," he said. "This will all make sense one day."

A buzzing noise startled me awake. I slammed my hand on the nightstand. It was my phone. Olivia shuffled on the bed as the noise continued. I glanced at the digital clock: 12:45 a.m. The number on the caller ID was a familiar one. It was the hospital.

I quickly sat up on the bed, the oxygen tubes on my face, a needle in my arm.

"Hello?" I took in a long breath. "Hello? Hello?"

"Paul." It was Dr. Brown. "I think you may be getting quite the gift today." I hoped my suspicion was true. "We have a heart."

Hearing those words caused an out-of-body experience.

"Still there?" she asked after my silence.

"Yes." I drew in a shuddering breath.

"Get here by two a.m., alright?"

"Okay!" I chuckled. "I'll see you soon."

Olivia stared with a gaping jaw, face still puffed. "Is it what I'm thinking?" she asked.

"Time for a Christmas heart."

She threw her arms around me and whispered, "You'll be fine. You have to be fine."

I called my sister Kirsten. She answered with a groggy voice but was fully alert when I broke the news. She agreed to stay with Neil and was at our doorstep in half an hour. We left as soon as she arrived, my parents meeting us at the hospital.

When it came to my feelings, I wasn't sure what to make of them. This was the only solution to keep me alive. And I could only get it by risking my life.

I was led to a room where the needle party began. A nurse hooked me up to a new IV. I had to shower to get rid of any bacteria before the surgery. Another nurse came into the shower and scrubbed me like I was a kid. I was perfectly capable of cleaning my-self, but they insisted on having a professional help me. Any small infection and I could wave this world goodbye.

A gray hospital gown was handed to me after she was done. The needle party continued after I changed. They drew four vials of blood in less than two minutes before leading me to a room where Olivia and my parents waited.

As I lay on the bed, I placed a hand over my chest and fol-lowed every single one of Sawyer's beats. Strangely, my chest tight-ened at the thought of losing my broken companion. He was to blame for the majority of my life's casualties, and even though he'd managed to teach me many lessons, Sawyer had to leave. The only part of him I would keep with me was his legacy.

Dad turned on the television, switching the channel until stumbling upon the news. The words coming from the news anchor were an echo in my head as thoughts of life and death waged a battle.

A knock on the door. Dr. Brown entered with a smile. Something glistened on her white coat as she approached. She had a pin shaped like a pine tree with the words *Merry Christmas* writ-ten across it.

A Merry Christmas indeed, I thought.

"Glad to see most of the family here," she said.

"Ready to do this, Doc," I said, holding up a fist.

"So are we. I just wanted to see you and say hello to the family. The anesthesiologist should be coming to get you in a few. See you soon."

Her last words were like a warning sign placed before a forked path. They meant life or death. This could very well be the last time I gathered with my family—or just one of many.

Tension settled after the doctor left. I knew everyone wanted to get a few words out in case this was the end. Since no one mustered the courage, I gulped in a sharp breath and said, "Mom, Dad, can you give me a moment with Olivia."

"Of course," Dad whispered.

Olivia came closer and sat on the edge of my bed. Her stare bore into me as if seeing my soul for the last time.

I held her hand and carefully scanned her face: her determined stare, her delicate lips, the hair falling over her ears. "Promise me if I—"

She said something in a gravelly voice I couldn't understand.

"I'm optimistic about all this," I continued. "But you—especially you—know the risks tonight. So in case—"

"You have to make it."

"If it's my time, promise you'll find the life you've always dreamed of." Her chin quivered. Her eyes glistened. "You deserve all the happiness in the world. I tried to be as normal as possible and create a normal life for us. For Neil. I know how much you dreamt of that. And there's no doubt you'll keep on being a great mom."

"I want to stay with you and raise our son," she said.

"When was the last time life asked us what we wanted?"

She gave me a tender kiss on the forehead. A tear dripped from her cheek to mine and rolled down my chin.

"Can you get my parents?" I asked.

She opened the door and left my parents and me alone.

Mom's cheeks were stained with her tears. Dad's face was serious, as if lost in thought.

"Thank you for everything," I said. "It hasn't been an easy road."

"One worth taking," Dad said.

They wheeled my bed out of the room at 5:20 a.m.

In the cold, brightly lit operating room, the nurses lifted me from my bed and laid me on the familiar narrow operating table. They were gowned and ready to cut me open. After being given a sedative to tame my anxiety, but before I was fully out, I was told everyone in the room needed to hear back from one of the surgeons who had gone to extract my donor's heart.

The waiting had the unexpected power to wipe the effects

of the sedative. What was taking so long? My mind was bombarded with thousands of reasons for the delay—none of them positive.

The phone on the wall rang. A nurse picked it up. I tried to eavesdrop on the conversation, but her words were distant whispers. She put the phone back and trudged closer to the bed. Even with half her face hidden behind a surgical mask, she wasn't able to conceal her worried stare.

"There was a problem with the heart," she said in a flat voice. "An aneurysm. They found it after it was removed."

I was having a nightmare. There was no way this was real.

"This might be your only chance, Paul." No, this wasn't a dream. "We can put the heart in, but you'll have to come back in a week to fix it. If it works." A pause. "Or you can keep waiting."

I searched for reason. Life had given me an ounce of hope only to steal back ten times as much. But it was Christmas. I wasn't going to die on my little boy today.

"I guess I'll keep on waiting," I said.

Acknowledgements

It's not everyday that one gets to work with one of their inspirations. I was already a fan way before I got to write this. Paul and Tina, thank you so much for entrusting me with this life-changing story. This journey has been my own broken miracle. I am forever grateful for your love and friendship.

To my incredible family, thank you for always cheering me on. You'll always be my inspiration to stay the path.

My legendary friends scattered across the globe, thank you for always keeping me grounded. Here's to many more adventures.

To every reader who has supported me in the past few years, thank you. You're the reason I get to keep on telling stories! Please forgive me for all the tears. You all know I am definitely not sorry for them though.

Last but definitely not least, I'm thankful that God has given me this platform. I will never take it lightly.

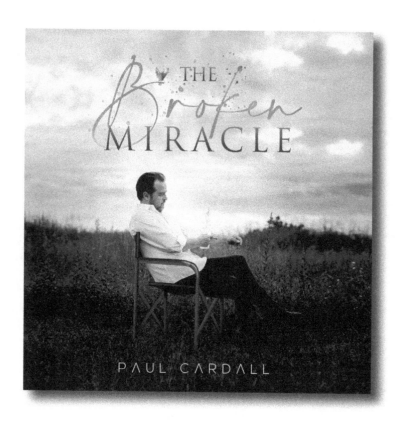

LISTEN TO THE MUSIC INSPIRED BY THE BROKEN MIRACLE.

Paul Cardall delivers a powerful soundtrack to the novel and his real life journey. The Broken Miracle album features special guests; David Archuleta, Tyler Glenn, Thompson Square, Rachael Yamagata, Ty Herndon, Matt Hammitt, Trevor Price, Akelee and Jordan Bratton. The Broken Miracle album is an invitation for the reader to dive deeper into the story.

TRACK LISTING

1. A Blue Baby
2. Moths & Butterflies
3. The Man With Half A Heart (Thompson Square)
4. Family
5. God & Religion
6. I Know It Hurts (Tyler Glenn)
7. A Beautiful Mind
8. All I See Is Snow (Thompson Square)
9. Our Children
10. For Better Or Worse
11. Change (Trevor Price)
12. My Heart Beats For You (David Archuleta)
13. Some Kind of Wonderful (Ty Herndon)
14. Finding My Way
15. Tina's Theme
16. Broken Machine (Rachael Yamagata)
17. The Broken Miracle (Matt Hammitt)
18. We Could Be Kind (Jordan Bratton, Akelee)
19. Epilogue

www.paulcardall.com